A Journey Within

Mark Douglas

 New Generation Publishing

*I would like to dedicate this book to my mother
Mrs Veronica Douglas, a lady who has dedicated her life
to her children and has asked for nothing in return.*

*This lady sacrificed her career and ultimately a chance
for a comfortable life. I thank you, Mum, for showing me
what it means to be selfless and understanding the true
value of the word 'sacrifice'.*

*May your journey into the next phase of your soul's
evolution be graceful and filled with love.*

Thank you for buying my book
the proceeds will go towards
helping my mother & sister on
Dominica an island in great
crisis after hurricane Maria.

[signature] Clark Douglas.

Contents

Prologue

What Came Before

It was Tuesday morning after the Christmas holidays when I arrived at work, I was late which was unusual for me. The main office had a strange air about it, devoid of the usual joking and happy cheer, I could see that some of the staff looked agitated.

Giving the matter little credence, I made my way to my office. Having just walked in and closed my door, I was interrupted by the office gossip, Tanya Grey, who burst into the room in a state of urgency.

Much to her excitement, Tanya informed me that our manager had been moved as a part of the company's restructure, and a new man had been put in charge. She went on to say that a meeting had been called and scheduled for midday.

I had already read the company statement in an email, so with nothing to add, I simply asked Tanya to close the door on her way out.

And that was the way I operated with most of the staff on a daily basis, an attitude that had also carried through to my personal life. This behaviour had developed from my childhood and throughout my school life, where I was subjected to name-calling and bullying. This had left me a loner, and the scars of distrust were now imbedded into my psyche. Naturally, my colleagues felt that I was too strange and avoided me as much as possible, leaving them to gossip about me.

The new manager, Chris Rodgers, had arrived shortly after me and introduced himself to the staff. By the time the meeting had begun, it was obvious that he was a ball-breaker and a trouble-shooter, which didn't concern me, as I always produced work over and above what was expected of me.

As he addressed the staff, it was clear that he was going to shake up the department and weed out the dead wood. After the meeting, a select few were called into his office, which didn't bother me, as I had a lot of work to be getting on with and I was far from what could be determined as a weak link.

It was four o'clock when I was locking the door to my office, as Chris rounded the corner:

"Ah, Antonia," he said. "Do you have a few minutes for me?"

"Well, I am just off home," I explained.

"That's OK, this will not take long," he said, making it quite clear that he had no interest in any other commitments that I might have.

Chris turned and I followed him to his office, as I glanced around the department, I could see that some of the staff were crying as they packed up their personal belongings. My meeting with Chris didn't fare any better. He ended the meeting by telling me:

"You have one of two choices, Antonia, find a desk on the main floor, or find a desk in a new job… either way I will have your office, so I suggest you deal with it. Now, if you don't mind, I have some phone calls to take care of, so please close the door on your way out."

I didn't sleep well that night. Chris had informed me that I had to be out of my office by Thursday to give it up to his personal secretary, which meant that I had no option but to move onto the main floor. I had been in his office for a little over half an hour arguing my case, which didn't go down too well with my new boss.

***

The months that followed put into motion a sequence of events that were to change my life forever. By the time July came, I found work to be unbearable. My approach to work was constantly scrutinised; this left me in a position where I began to question my position in the business, which I believed had come as a direct consequence of my argument with Chris way back in January.

At seventeen, I had tried to take my own life and I still had the scars to prove it. Now, at thirty-five, I was travelling down that dark road once again, and the feeling of depression was slowly creeping in on me with every passing day.

By September, it seemed that my work had little value to me or to my manager, and I knew that I had to get on top of this situation if I was to keep my sanity… *what little sanity I had left.*

Anxiety had taken hold. It was now triggered by the mere sight of Chris. Clearly, something had to be done, and done quickly. I had been to counselling after I had tried to commit suicide, at the time I felt that it was not helping, so against the doctors' wishes I stopped my therapy in its infancy. As time progressed I developed a single-minded attitude that served me well throughout my working life but I now discovered that I was unable to stand up for myself and was allowing my boss to control me.

I decided to take the plunge, I did some research that I hoped would put a stop to this constant flow of negativity, and found a psychiatrist by the name of Eugene Graham, his advertisement caught my eye and I felt that if anybody, he could help me regain control over my life once again.

Chapter One

The Awakening

It was a Saturday afternoon when I made my first appointment to see my psychiatrist, Dr Eugene Graham. I saw this as an opportunity finally to get my life back on track. At the initial interview, the doctor devised a strategy that would consist of weekly visits, costs, and an estimate of how long he perceived it would take to gain some semblance of normality into my life.

After six visits at the psychiatrist's, it seemed that little progress had been made, Dr Graham could sense the frustration in me, so a new approach was thought up which I reluctantly agreed to. I was extremely sceptical about this approach as I had heard negative reports of hypnotherapy, but given that I was so desperate for a successful outcome, I was willing to try anything.

The first four sessions seemed to be a huge disappointment to both my doctor and myself, as no tangible improvements had been made. There were times when I would simply fall asleep during the sessions. However, the doctor was persistent in his endeavours to help me, and on the fifth visit, we had a breakthrough. Having gone under deep hypnosis, I found myself travelling to a distant past.

I heard the voice of Dr Graham bringing me through the preparation process and I became very relaxed. Nevertheless, before he could fully get into his programme, I started speaking in a tone that was unrecognisable to him. Eugene had heard of cases where the patient had slipped into a past life, but he had never experienced it first-hand. However, he allowed it to continue, and what followed was truly remarkable.

Through carefully selected questions, I was able to describe my surroundings, my feelings, my interactions...

all from the life that I was living whilst under deep hypnosis. The questions continued until Eugene was satisfied that the correct parameters were set.

"Who are you?" Eugene asked.

"My name is Aglaia," I said.

"How old are you?" he asked.

"I am five years old."

"What are you doing, Aglaia?"

"I can hear my mother calling out to me. It's time to eat, and I am playing in the gardens with my friends… animals large and small, old and new-borns alike, but the most beloved of all is a lioness. I call her Maeja, which means mother. I have known her since my birth and she is my guardian."

"How is it that you can play with such an animal as this?"

"In this land when some people are born they are born with a gift to communicate with the animals by way of their minds. From birth, it is known which one of us has the ability to communicate with animals. Of those few, some are united with an animal that they are linked to at a birthing ceremony. These animals become their companions and guardians," under hypnosis the words, thoughts and visions came through so naturally and clearly I felt that I was actually there, which was not too far from the truth.

"The animal that the infant will be paired with is chosen specifically through a series of visions given to the high priestess, instruction is given to the high priestess to connect the soul of the infant to the soul of their animal and guide. What follows is a ritual that in time I will become familiar with. The presence of the real animal solidifies our link with our spirit animal. A priest of the order of record keepers performs this ceremony. However, not all Atlanteans have this honour bestowed on them, for the great crystal can somehow sense the power of the individual's soul and instructs the high priestess of what needs to be done and what animal is destined for the person in question. When the ceremony is complete, the animal is left to live with the infant and there they stay until they pass on."

Eugene was convinced that my visions were authentic, and this experience was not a chance occurrence. Each time I went under deep hypnosis, I would find myself picking up from where I had left off, in a world far different from our own. From the moment that Eugene realised what was happening he instinctively began to record our sessions. I would continue to see Eugene for over three years and although improvements were seen, it was decided to continue the journey that we had started. This is my accounting of a life I once lived, in a distant land, in a distant past long forgotten.

***

Our meals consisted mainly of fruit, leaves and the roots of the earth, these were left in their natural place of growth until they were needed. We would only take what we could consume. We would sit where our spirit took us, we would then bless the food and thank our providers. Our animals, if we were blessed with one, would join us. They were known as our guardians or companions, but to me Maeja was my friend and my family.

At our meal time, we would talk about our visions and dreams, this time could be best described as a gathering of minds. This was a beautiful time where everything was discussed. Animals would also join the conversation using telepathy; however, they were only linked with their partners.

My parents would often tell me and Maeja to take better care with our thoughts, as I would often find myself laughing at inappropriate moments due to Maeja's humour.

As I grew older, I found more people taking an interest in me. Occasionally, I would be asked questions or be involved in lengthy discussions with a young initiate from the temple, whose visits were becoming more frequent. On one occasion I had even spoken to an elderly man, who I was to learn was the grandmaster. Our conversations at meal times grew deeper, at times it seemed that I was being tested by the gentleman but more importantly it seemed that the information that I was supplying was coming from a place that was not a part of my existence. In these meetings we would discuss my views on all manner of things including what I thought my future might be. It was during these talks that I began to feel that I was destined for greatness.

Maeja began to understand this also. She was loyal to me; as she grew she flourished into the most powerful and majestic guardian. She was protective yet gentle, and so full of wisdom, she would only leave my side when she needed to feed. On many of our lengthy walks we would have deep discussions on what we had learnt from our visitors, and at times I would often wonder where Maeja's wisdom was coming from, as I did with my own knowledge.

On my fifteenth deliverance day, I arrived home to find the grandmaster and a lady that I had never seen before in the gardens with my parents. The lady had her guardian with her. Maeja and I walked confidently up to them and took our places. The grandmaster turned to me, and with a gracious smile he asked, "Do you know why we are here?"

I looked at Maeja and then at the lady with much thought, as I concentrated I began to see.

"Hermione is going to train me for the temple of light," I said calmly. "I am to become the giver of light." They both looked surprised.

"I left strict instruction that my name was never to be uttered; how did you come to know it?" The lady was firm but gentle with her approach.

"Maeja and I know it to be so."

"How do you know such things?" the lady asked.

"The crystal told us."

"What crystal, young lady?"

"Why the Great Crystal of course."

The grandmaster held his place and said nothing, as it was clear that he answered to the lady.

"What do you know of this crystal?" she continued.

"I know that the crystal is closely linked to you."

"And what does your lioness say about the matter?"

"She says to play your game; she also says that you have a beautiful soul." Hermione laughed as did the grandmaster.

"You have exceeded all our hopes and dreams of all that has been set out before you. You have also surpassed all others that have been tested before you."

The grandmaster now interrupted by touching the lady on her arm. "It is time."

At that point, we all got up to leave, that was the last I would see of my parents until I was needed by them for their passing-on ceremony. We then left for the temple to start my training, or so I thought.

Hermione, would not grow to be my teacher, but she would become a close and beloved friend. On her shoulder nested the largest eagle I had ever seen; it was her guardian and her name was Liya.

"Aigle, what do you know of the training you are to undergo?" Hermione said softly.

"The training takes as long as is required, I will be tested on my ability to stay true to the nature of the temple of light. After my cleansing ceremony, you will give my name to me. If I achieve mastery over my emotions, I will be reborn under my new name, which will be linked to my responsibility in the temple. And just to be clear, my name is Aglaia." *Another test*, I thought.

"My apologies, but I needed to know how assertive you are. Have you had any visions of your role in the temple?"

I looked at Maeja and smiled. "In time I will be taking your place as high priestess."

Hermione returned the smile: "You are more intuitive than I was at your age. It pleases me, for we have a short time before I leave. As for your training, you do not require any, as the great crystal shall be your guide and instructor."

"Do you believe the Lemurians can change?" I asked.

There was a small level of surprise in her eyes, and an admiration for the fact that I was aware of her plans… this was something she had not discussed with anybody.

The thought had entered Hermione's mind about the Lemurians. However, a greater force was driving her; she had seen the vision of her assisting the Lemurians, and it was forbidden to question a vision given to you from the great crystal.

"The Lemurians are our cousins and it is my duty to assist those that want our help. However, for some I fear that it is too late for them to change; there are some Lemurians who have abused the gifts and abilities that have been bestowed on them. This abuse is creating negativity in their civilization; such negativity will destroy their lands."

As Hermione was expressing her thoughts regarding the Lemurians I could now feel intense sorrow in her voice.

The high priestess of the temple holds the highest honour of all Atlanteans, even higher than that of the grandmaster. The high priestess of the light commanded all the power, knowledge, memories, and energy that the great crystal holds, as Hermione put it, "It is a sharing of knowledge."

This was explained to me by Hermione as we walked through the gardens towards the temple; this was followed by Hermione giving us a very basic understanding of the responsibilities that she holds. "The crystals are a powerhouse of knowledge, memories and energy, it is a great responsibility, as high priestess I oversee most if not all ceremonies. Initiation into the temple is a long process, which can take years to achieve mastery and longer to reach the position of highness." Hermione spoke with humility and pride, so much so that I could see it in her eyes.

Finally, we reached the temple, Maeja and I were shown to our chamber, which was small and sparse; it had a table, a stool and a bed. Maeja found her spot and lay down, I sat on my stool to take in my new surroundings.

"I will leave you now," the high priestess said. "For tomorrow you will be taken to the cleansing chamber where your journey will begin. May the love of the creator be with you, my child."

With that said I was left alone. Maeja and I spent the rest of that evening discussing what was to be our new home, there were times of serious talk but mostly we kept to our age and had fun.

Chapter Two

The Rebirth

It was early morning when two priestesses came to our chamber. I was already prepared for their arrival, as I had slept well but woke early due to the immense excitement that filled my body. The two priestesses that entered my room looked at me with a gentle smile but said nothing, I knew I was to follow them; as we left for the cleansing chamber two more joined us from behind, also in silence, leaving Maeja to bring up the rear, we all knew our place... I could feel Maeja's eagerness and curiosity growing inside of her.

The chamber that we entered was dome-shaped with a central disk floor, surrounded by five pillars. At the top of the dome was a large rose quartz crystal, in front of each pillar was a smaller crystal of blue quartz. Lining the walls of the chamber were all the priestesses of the temple of light, they were dressed in white robes and wore golden masks. In one hand they held a rose quartz crystal, and in the other a lantern with a pleasant aroma of burning oils which left trails of smoke around the chamber.

My four companions took up their places, Maeja sat at the entrance and I took my place on the disk in the centre of the dome. Hermione entered the chamber and stood next to Maeja, without a word uttered they both made their way towards me. Hermione stopped at the edge of the disk, Maeja bowed her head to her and then joined me on the disk. Hermione walked around the outside of the circle blessing each pillar as she passed them. With each blessing the blue crystal began to vibrate, as it did, it emitted a gentle tone... once Hermione had completed the circle, she held out her arms and turned to face me.

"I, Hermione, protector and mother to the temple of light, ask our brothers and sisters – the crystals – to join with us in this blessing. We welcome the child Aglaia, and her companion Maeja into your circle. Wash and purify their souls. Allow their light to become our light, and allow our light to become theirs. This is the way it has always been and always will be. My daughters, lift up your light now and welcome these two beautiful souls into our light."

And with that the priestesses raised their heads and arms and emitted a sound that seemed to come from the deepest part of their beings, this matched the harmonic vibration of the crystals. Then the most wondrous thing happened; the crystals fired out a beam of light, each crystal was connected by this light, then each crystal simultaneously shot their light up to the top centre crystal, which then joined the choir and shot a beam of light down into the centre of my crown. Instantly, I was lifted from the ground and I could feel the power of the crystals surging through me but no pain. I could also feel the presence of a greater power, in that moment my body shone as if it were pure energy. That was when I became one with the great crystal. The true core of the temple of light.

Maeja roared and I could see that she was also glowing. Slowly, I was lowered down onto the disk, and everybody bowed their heads. The cleansing was complete, the priestesses began to leave the room in two's, then me, Maeja and Hermione, followed by ten more. As we walked, Hermione took this time to speak with me.

"All are pleased. You have been accepted by the great crystal, she is not of this world and was gifted to us by beings far greater than we can imagine. We have been charged with the duty of protecting her, for there are those who desire to use her for their own personal gain."

"I sensed this when I connected with the crystal; you said she, so the crystal has a personality." A concept that I had not considered until that time. "I could see its journey through the stars, sorry I should say her. The race of people who gifted her to us, and the fact that they are still connected to her. They will one day return for her."

"Yes, you speak the truth, for they know that the will of man is weak, and in time you will learn just how much of a personality she has." Hermione seemed more than pleased with my connection.

We had reached our destination, it was the robing chamber; there was a bowl of water in the centre of the room scented with flowers, some drying cloths, a white robe was nested on a bench, and next to the robe was a bracelet with a small crystal nested in its centre. The priestesses removed the clothes I was wearing, washed and dressed me in my new robe. Hermione placed my bracelet on my wrist, she then turned to Maeja, looked gently into her eyes and gently said to her. "Take me where we need to go."

Now it was Maeja's turn to take the lead; the priestesses had already left the chamber and now it was just the three of us.

"Why are we alone?" I asked.

"We are going to a special place that only four souls know about. You need to understand, Aglaia, that Maeja was born in this chamber, I was guided here by way of a vision, and on my arrival, Maeja's mother was sitting in wait for me. She was not raised as a guardian and had never been around people. I could feel this, yet I wasn't afraid of her as I knew that this day was destined. This is one of the reasons why I can also communicate with Maeja. Aglaia, you must also know that when all this has finished, you will have the ability to communicate with all things if you wish it."

We stopped in front of a wall as Hermione continued her story:

"Maeja's mother placed her paws on this very wall, I knew I had to follow and on the placing of my hands, the wall seemed to vanish and we were in another room. The room where Maeja was born. This was my introduction to a part of the crystal that has remained closed to all until your birth."

"You said four know of this place," I said.

"Yes. Maeja, her mother, myself, and the original guardian, who is not of this world. She trained the priestesses and formed the temple of light, and this was her chamber, this is where she would come to commune with her people."

Both Maeja and I knew that we needed to duplicate what was just explained to us, as we did we found ourselves standing in the centre of the room yet we did not seem to move. Again, the room was a dome with a single quartz crystal, on one of the walls was the painting of the matriarch. Standing beside her, was a lion with a golden headpiece – her guardian – and all the high priestesses that had served in Atlantis.

"Hermione, that symbol above the matriarch... I have seen this around the temple. What does it mean?" I asked.

"That, my child, is the symbol of the matriarch. It is the symbol of the planet of her birth, and a constant reminder for all who serve the temple that this place originated from superior beings."

On a small pillar was the golden headpiece from the picture on the wall, I could see that it was worn by the first lion; it was more like a crown. At the centre of it was a small crystal, identical to the one on my bracelet. Hermione could see that the crystals had taken my attention.

"The bracelet and headpiece have not been worn by any other, apart from the matriarch and her guardian, they are brother and sister and have not been together for an age. Today that has all changed."

As I looked at Maeja, I could instantly see that the lion was now her. His soul had been reincarnated into her body, and reborn as my faithful guardian. I looked at Hermione and with a tear in my eye I expressed what I was feeling. "Am I to be the last?"

"Yes, my sweet child, and you are a child no more. You are now reborn, as such it is left to me to give you your name, you will now be known as Gaia, the mother of the temple of light."

She knelt down and Maeja placed her paw on her shoulder, for the first time, I could hear Hermione and Maeja speak telepathically. I focused my mind and listened to what Hermione had to say.

"It has been an honour to have helped give you life, and watch you grow. You have protected Gaia, and with your help and guidance she has become who she was destined to be. For that, I am grateful."

Hermione then offered up a prayer to the great Crystal. "Please impart in me the power and strength for the journey ahead, for now it is I who needs your guidance." Hermione was humble and gracious. But it was Maeja who gave Hermione the response.

"It has been given to me to place in you the wisdom of all that has come before us. Let it give you strength in your hours of weakness, and give you light in your darkest times."

In that moment, I knew in my heart, after that night I would never see Hermione again.

Hermione took the headpiece and placed it on Maeja's head. It was a perfect fit and I was not surprised. Since the time of the cleansing ceremony, Maeja seemed to be larger and more majestic, we were both finally in our rightful places. Upon placing the headpiece on Maeja, the crystal in it and my bracelet began radiating beams of light, and as they joined, our bond grew. I felt a flood of ancient memories fill my very existence. I now understood that our bond was not constrained by time or earthly troubles. We were now as one, a single entity that only the infinite wisdom of stars could comprehend. I could have wept, were I not overcome with awe. As this happened the chain securing the crystal appeared to merge into Maeja's skin.

When the process came to an end, all that was visible was the crystal, I asked Maeja: "Did you feel any pain?"

"No I did not although I was fully aware of what was happening."

I turned to Hermione: "How is this possible?"

raised up on her hind legs and placed her two front paws on each door. As she did so, the doors took on a slight glow and they began to unbolt all on their own. They then slowly opened.

"Blessed be," the high priestess said. "The final test is passed; their hearts are as one, and they are pure."

She had to see if I would intuitively open the door, or if I would blindly try to open it in a conventional manner. When the doors opened, those who were present entered, leaving the three of us outside.

"As you know," Hermione continued, "An initiate goes through vigorous training with priests and priestesses alike. Then, after years of service, they hope to aspire to become a high priestess. Only two people have ever risen to the highest position of our order so quickly. You are the only high priestess that has come into being without having to go through the difficult tests of initiation. You are the only one to pass the final test of acceptance with such ease and grace. Great things are expected of you, Gaia, great things indeed."

The central chamber was majestic in appearance. The walls and floor were made of marble, with twelve marble pillars etched in gold.

Levitating from a central position was the largest crystal I had ever seen. Hermione took one last look at the gathering and then looked at me. Now she was not smiling, her face was gentle but controlled and very serious, she turned and faced both Maeja and I, then touched our cheeks. "This is my final act as high priestess," and without saying any more, she walked gracefully towards the centre of the marble circle of pillars, took her place, then turned to face me and pronounced in a voice that commanded power, force and respect.

"I, Hermione, am no more, from this day forth I am now of my deliverance day name, I am Ourania. Your mother has been born anew. Your mother is now Gaia, love her, embrace her, as you have done for me, she is now high priestess of the temple of light. I now give back to the great crystal what she has given to me with love and adoration, with all the wisdom that I have gathered, so she may pass it on to Gaia, my successor." With that, Ourania closed her eyes and rose off the ground. What I can only describe as a part of her soul was lifted out of her body in the form of an energy wave, and went into the crystal. She remained frozen in this position. With her arms outstretched and her head gazing towards the heavens, she looked so beautiful.

I could hear the Great Crystal whispering to me. Maeja could hear it too. "Gaia, it's your time now, come into my embrace and accept what is yours by rite of passage."

I now knew that I had to take Hermione's body and give her back to the order of light. The room was focused on me and Maeja, I then calmly entered the ring of pillars, walked up to her and it seemed as if the Great Crystal placed her into my arms. As I took her, the two eldest priests came to the edge of the circle, but did not enter. Ourania felt extremely light. I held her body out to them and they took her out of the circle and then retreated. Maeja came over to join me and on her arrival, we were both lifted by the crystal. A cloud of energy surrounded us, engulfed us, then entered into us, filling our whole essence with the full record of all who have been called high priestess. All their secrets, their conversations, their actions, absolutely nothing was left out. I could see it all, I could feel the power, the energy coursing through my body. It was truly beautiful and I could understand why this great crystal needed to be protected. I felt energized and majestic and I saw all this in the blink of an eye, and through our bond I could feel that Maeja too had all this which I had become; we were truly one.

By the time this process was over Ourania had fully recovered, the crystal had restored her to her former self, but had given her the gift of remembrance, strength, and all the power that she held as high priestess. For we who had knowledge, knew that she would need it for the times ahead. I could see in her eyes that although the return to her former self had shaken her, I knew she was going to be okay. I gently came back to the ground, thanked the crystal for choosing us and addressed the people who were now my children:

"Children of the light, I have been chosen by the great crystal to be your next mother. I have been reborn as Gaia, protector of the Great Central Crystal. The knowledge and strength of our forbearers has been gifted to my guardian and me, until it is my time. This is how it was in days past, and how it will always be. This is the will of the creator, blessed be."

Everyone present came before me and bowed, as they did they addressed me as "Gaia mother of the light". Finally, Ourania bowed, Ourania was last she addressed me but after bowing she took my arm and for the first time we walked arm in arm.

"You know I will not be coming back," she explained.

"Yes," I said. "I also noticed that the high priest was absent."

"Yes, his journey has left him bitter and confused as to the nature of his position."

I looked at her with a high level of sympathy, for I knew she would be sacrificing her life for the benefit of our world.

"I have no regrets," she said, she could see my thoughts. "I have seen and experienced many wonders and I would not change a thing. I know you understand, and in time, your sacrifice will come to pass also."

Yes, I thought, I already knew that to be true, as did Maeja.

"We have one more thing to do, but for now, we will travel in silence, I have become weary and wish to reflect on what has come to pass," Ourania said.

***

We had arrived back at the chamber, now Ourania felt free

to speak.

"This place is the most highly protected area in this kingdom," Ourania explained as we entered the hidden chamber. "In here, all can be discussed as you wish. You may speak with your mind or with your body. This is how the matriarch, our benefactor, communicated with her people. In here, you can talk with the great crystal if she wills it. We have both learned of the priest's dissatisfaction in his position and of his desire to have more. This is the reason why women have always been the only ones to hold the light. He wishes to change things. He was most angered that your ascension was kept from him. So, to show his disapproval, he chose to be absent at the passing over of power, for he knew that his anger would not have been tolerated by the crystal. She is wise and will only let a pure heart enter the central chamber during the rite of passage ceremony. I understand that you have many questions. You must learn patience, Gaia, all will come to you in time but I do know that she was pleased that you picked up on his energy, and in time your abilities and knowledge will grow stronger."

"She? Do you mean the great crystal?" I asked. Ourania smiled.

"Yes, she will help you and Maeja to learn to protect your thoughts, which will be invaluable in the weeks to come as you begin to pay attention to those around you. You now have the ability and power to listen to people's thoughts, so train your mind to become vigilant. I will bring you to my two most trusted priestesses and friends. Ianthe is to be my companion and she has been told merely that we are going to see some old friends; the other is Timo, who I have been training since your birth to assist you from this day forward."

"I have met Timo at my house," I said.

"Yes, she was the one who helped you and your parents through your training. They are my most trusted friends and confidantes, so put your trust and faith in her and she will serve you well."

"If this is true, why is she not going with you?"

"You need to understand that Timo was chosen at birth by the great crystal, as only she can see all paths set out before all souls, she gave me the vision of what to do, how to train her, and how she was to help you. Timo was brought to the temple at a young age and she was raised to be yours and yours alone."

Our last moments together were spent walking through the gardens. There were no goodbyes, as we knew that we would communicate through our dreams by way of the crystal. Ourania was gone the following morning.

***

The priestesses were the keepers of the light, while the priests were the keepers of records, they performed the birthing, naming and the passing over ceremonies. The high priest of the order was a formidable man, and it was clear that he had his own agenda, not only that but also he was one to watch. Ourania had warned me that he desired more than what was fitting of his station, and of late he had been pushing hard for use of the great crystal in the birthing ceremony. As he put it, "It will give you time to do other things."

He would soon use this same argument to try to sway me into allowing him access to the great crystal. However, I knew there was more to it than that. This was backed up in time by the great crystal, a fact that I was already beginning to see. Ourania only gave me what was needed at the time, as she knew the crystal would keep me well informed.

Our communications between Maeja, the crystal and I grew more frequent, through it I was soon to understand that he felt that he had learnt how to shield himself from the great crystal. More importantly he had also learnt how to grow and design his own crystals, a fact that Maeja had discovered on one of her hunting trips.

She was in the forest and picked up his scent.

"Gaia, the high priest is here and I feel that he is not doing temple business."

"Follow him and keep me informed," I said. "I will ask the crystal to mask your approach."

The crystal was already on that mission, "Not to worry, Gaia. I masked her as soon as she left the temple."

During our communications, I learnt that the great crystal was called Hypatia, who also had a sense of humour. However, the high priest was becoming a problem.

"We of the high command have known that this time would come, and it must come to pass," Hypatia explained. This was the first time I heard Hypatia mention or hint at any other presence other than what was on the earth. From that point on, I became closer to Hypatia, who was truly akin to my mother.

Together we were quite a team, and between the three of us, we grew stronger with each passing day. I was well respected and trusted within the temple. We performed the passing over ceremonies, joining ceremonies, oversaw the naming ceremonies, healings, land cleansings. The list was immense but we prevailed. With Hypatia's help, we learnt how to meditate whilst still performing our duties and it seemed that temple life was not affected by the change of the high priestess.

Six months had passed when I heard my first communication from Ourania; she had reached the land of the Lemurians.

Chapter Three

Ourania

Ourania set off at the crack of dawn, however if there was ever a reason for her to stay in Atlantis, this particular sunrise would have done it, set against the bay it was truly a sight to see. Ourania and her companion wore plain street clothes, this was a direct request of not only the captain but the great crystal as well. In the weeks that proceeded Ourania's departure, she had made arrangements with a sea captain called Leonidas, who had been recommended to her by the grandmaster and confirmed by the great crystal. He was a man of honour and owed the grandmaster a debt, and to his credit he wanted no payment in his words.

"It is my duty to serve the high priestess. My arm is yours and your life is for me to protect, for I owe the grandmaster a debt, which I am now happy to repay." The sea captain was good to his word.

When Ourania and Ianthe arrived at the docks, Captain Leonidas and his crew were ready to greet them. At Ourania's request, on their first meeting she had asked Leonidas not to reveal their identity to his crew until they were clear of Atlantis. Captain Leonidas protested, and spoke proudly of his crew's loyalty and asked why the need for deception. Leaving Ourania with no option but to show him the power of the people that was close to the temple, with a little demonstration that she hoped would give Leonidas the mindset to understand her reasons.

"It is not your crew's loyalty that concerns me."

To make sure the captain understood her reasons, Ourania re-enforced this with a demonstration of her powers.

"Leonidas, you are the only son of a fisherman called Iovilios, who wanted you to join the priesthood, however you loved the sea. You had a partner who you loved dearly but she was taken from you too soon, in a despicable way, a fact that you still refuse to speak of. From that day forward you devoted your life to the sea, helping all that is in your power to help. Yes, you do trust your crew; it is not your crew that we watch, it is another. And as you can see we have ways of obtaining knowledge without having to ask for it, for this very reason, I ask for your silence."

Captain Leonidas was impressed. He had heard of the gifts of the temple, but to witness them was a lesson well received. He thanked her for sharing that with him, and from that moment she had earned his respect.

As the ship started its voyage, Ourania felt a familiar presence, and smiled as she turned to see Maeja sitting on the docks watching them leave. "You have been with us since we left the temple have you not, Maeja."

"Yes, Ourania, I was sent by the great crystal to watch over you."

"Was my safety in question?"

"Your safety has been in question for many days now, I have been watching over you from afar."

"Oh, that does not surprise me, yet while I felt a presence, it is strange that I did not know it was you."

"The Great Crystal masked my identity; this was done to warn you. It is possible for thoughts and intentions of others to be hidden, possibly even from the great crystal. It seems that the priest has worked on perfecting this skill and he feels that he has been successful. Until recently, only the great crystal has had this knowledge; however, there are others on this planet who can boast to have obtained such knowledge. As you can imagine, this is a very dangerous period, and one that leaves me unclear as to how much time we really have. I have been informed that you will be meeting people that have such abilities."

"Thank you, Maeja," Ourania said, "and thank you, Hypatia."

"Do you know that majestic lion, priestess?" Captain Leonidas asked.

"Yes, Leonidas, she is a very good friend of mine. She has come to say goodbye and she would not be happy to hear you say lion, as she is a lioness."

"Atlanteans," he laughed. "I could never get my head around how they get on with animals, and a thousand apologies to you, lioness."

Maeja roared in acknowledgement. "She thanks you for your recognition," Ourania said.

***

Leonidas was not native to these shores but he embraced their culture and had proven himself to be a trustworthy man; his crew were loyal and protective over him, mainly because ninety percent of them owed him their lives in one way or another. Some were orphans or beggars, some had appointments with executioners, but all had a story to tell that always finished with Leonidas clutching them out of the jaws of a one-way fate, they named him the collector of men, a fitting name.

Atlantean priestesses and priests were not people of the sea, the closest we ever came to it was if we needed to heal a person using the life force that the sea provides. In our healings, we use what nature and the great crystal directs us to use; we do not question, for to question is to doubt, and to have doubt makes you question the foundation on which trust and faith are built on. To do that would destroy the very nature of our existence, and our connection to all that is. Ourania on her first day of the voyage felt that the food that she had consumed earlier that day was having a strange effect on her equilibrium,

"Captain, I do not understand this, have I been poisoned?"

"Goddess, be praised," he said. "Blessed priestess, you are suffering from land disease. It is a term us sea folk use when a land-based person joins a sea voyage for the first time. It will pass when you become accustomed to how she moves. We believe the sea is a living force that if she is not respected she will put you in harm's way. If you lie down and close your eyes, she will calm you, and she may even talk to you if you are willing to listen, but this uneasiness that you feel will pass."

Following Leonidas's advice, Ourania and Ianthe began to feel better. The voyage was set to be a very long one, with no land to be seen for many weeks. There was plenty of food to eat, however, Ourania and Ianthe refused to eat any flesh, much to the amusement of the crew, a fact that Leonidas wanted to put a stop to.

"My friends," Captain Leonidas called his crew together, he was now ready to chastise his crew for their lack of respect. "Have you not wondered why I choose not to mock these ladies; in fact, why I treat them with such reverence. These two ladies are the high priestess and priestess of the temple of light, so for those of us who are not worldly wise, it means that they have the power invested in them to do magical things… things that would have you in pain. So, as a cautionary note, I suggest that you afford these kind ladies a bit of respect."

The crew looked around at each other, and burst out in fits of laughter. Leonidas leaned over to Ourania and said quietly.

"If you indeed know of any trickery that would help to bolster my claim, now would be a very good time to give a small demonstration."

"You have a child's mind, Leonidas, I will play your game if not for amusement."

Ourania looked up at the sky in search of her friend and guardian Liya, who she had asked to keep her distance until she was needed. At night, she would rest on the tallest mast and Ourania would come to see her when everybody was asleep.

Ourania called for Liya who flew down and landed on her shoulder.

The sailor that had the most to say blurted out, "Look, the lady has brought us lunch."

Although Ourania knew in his heart he was just

mocking, both she and Liya turned to look at him menacingly, the crew burst out with laughter even Leonidas cracked a smile but tried to stay with the theme of the mood. The man continued to mock them nevertheless.

"Maybe the bird will dance for us," he called out. Ourania and Liya had a link and bond much like Maeja and myself, strong and true. Ourania and Liya faced each other again and as Ourania was telling her what she wanted her to do, her tormentor spoke out again.

"Oh, he is going to get his," Liya exclaimed, which made Ourania smile for she knew Liya had a streak in her that was true to her nature.

She flew to the floor by Ourania's foot, bowed and walked over to the captain, and bowed to him. With a swagger, she walked up to the offending sailor, and then drove her beak into his leg and calmly walked away. The crew were in awe of what they had seen, but erupted into fits of laughter. As for the now shamed crewman, he was not too pleased, he put his hand on the hilt of his sword, but before he had a chance to draw his sword, his hand on the hilt, Ourania stepped forward and proclaimed in a voice and manner that comes purely from a point of protection and a connection to higher powers.

"Before you have a chance to strike out at my companion, I suggest you look over my shoulder. Swimming in the distance is a beast which I have contacted, I believe you call this particular animal a shark, and I can call out to a variety of other sea creatures to pull you into the sea."

With that, as if on cue, the sea started to churn. The sailor did indeed see the fin of the shark and calmly took his hand off the hilt of the sword.

"Now you might want to apologise to Liya for threatening to have her for lunch, or she might make this passage a difficult one for you."

This made the crew roar out with laughter, the captain too.

"Lucky for the bird you were here," the sailor said through gritted teeth. Now they all laughed, the apology was made and the two became good friends, although the sailor was reluctant to admit it.

After that the crew began to come to the ladies for all manner of problems and advice, on one occasion Ianthe expressed to Ourania:

"It's like being at the temple, priestess."

No matter how hard Ourania had tried, she could not get her out of the habit of calling her that. The ladies were not accustomed to being a burden to anybody, as such they took on all manner of chores for they were determined not to be ornaments. If Leonidas was not going to allow them to pay for their passage, then they were going to earn their way to Lemuria. Even Liya earned her way as she was a master when it came to fishing, she and their tormentor would often be seen at the side of the ship, him with his rod and Liya watching until he hooked his prey. At first she would torment him. She would wait till his prey was tired and ready to be landed when she would fly down steal his catch and fly up to the top mast to which he would scream, cuss and curse, to the utter amusement of the crew. Then when he thought that she had tired of this game, she would wait for him to land his catch, he would look at Liya with pride and then say to her, "Now beat that if you can," which she always did.

By the time the ship had reached land the ladies were as much a part of the crew. There were even some eyes full of water well-hidden, but there none the less. As for their tormentor, he and Liya had become the perfect double act, and close friends, he even kissed her crown and said goodbye. The ladies said their goodbyes to the crew and Ourania asked Captain Leonidas if she could use his services again, to which he was more than happy to assist her. "I will send my friend to you and you will know when to come," Ourania explained.

"But how will you know where to find me?" he asked.

"With all that you have seen these past months, you ask

me a question like that," she said, and they both laughed.

The ladies left the ship and made their way inland, finding a place to rest where they waited for Ourania's counterpart to arrive.

Ourania and her counterpart had been in contact on several occasions by way of visions, aided by Hypatia. Everything had been arranged for Ourania's arrival, and due to the nature of the visit, the fewer people that were aware the better. After all, there were those who had caused irreparable damage to the planet, and as such, the earth needed protecting.

In Atlantis, only those most trusted in the temple knew of the link with outer world visitors, and as far as Ourania knew, Atlantis was the only place where such an event has ever happened.

The Lemurians had a connection to the earth and they understood her, much like our association to the great crystal. They lived in harmony, yet throughout the passage of time many had forgotten about their link to the earth mother.

In time, Ourania would discover that, and much more.

"It is time, Ianthe," Ourania said. "He is here."

Chapter Four

The High Priest

Bion was a tall man, who was slender and handsome for his mature age. His head was shaved and he dressed in plain clothes. He had been deposed, this was an action that was unheard of for people such as us, which put him in unfamiliar territory, people in our position usually served until we passed on, or hand over the mantle of responsibility, much like Ourania and myself.

However, since it was not only forced but unnatural, Bion was still connected to the power that was bestowed onto him, as a result, his life was in constant danger. There had been several failed attempts on Bion's life, but because he was still a high priest and keeper for the earth, his connection to the earth and its spiritual soul meant that he was protected from assassination with the help of some extremely gifted individuals. These individuals would help him to see his would-be assassins, also due to his link to the earth he was able to reach out to Ourania to ask her for assistance and guidance with the help of the great crystal and another entity that kept itself eluded from Ourania's sight. Ourania and Bion would often receive detailed visions that helped with matters of importance between each other in their sleep, this ensured that the protection of the planet was always paramount. Plans were drawn up for the integration of the knowledge shared by the two civilisations; however, before they could be put into action, he was overthrown.

This was not perceived as being a problem, in fact it played into Bion's hand quite nicely, as this gave him time to prepare for the arrival of Ourania. He was made aware for my progression, so when my time arrived to become the new priestess of Atlantis, he was very excited as this made it possible for Ourania to travel.

is best for us and for our planet, in doing so, they are violating the planet's sacredness and natural patterns, this is causing her pain."

"This is truly remarkable, please continue."

"The earth-mother, as we like to call her, has blessed me with information that must be shared. And while this is a good location, it is not as safe as it used to be. So, let's gather your belongings and be on our way," Bion said with an air of caution in his voice.

Ourania instructed Liya to fly high and inform her if people were close by, although she could sense people's energy, the lesson learnt from Hypatia and Maeja served her well, and she was always cautious from that moment on.

They walked under the cover of the forest for the entire day without rest. Ourania could tell Bion was anxious to get to the place that was to become their home. She didn't question his haste or try to slow his pace, although she was feeling a little short of breath; Ourania did not have the advantage of youth like Ianthe, the life she left behind saw her daily activities at a much gentler pace. As they walked, Bion had indeed noticed that Ourania was becoming, as he put it, "well exercised." Ourania smiled and knew that he was trying to be kind. Now Ourania could sense that he was being distracted as he walked, his pace had not altered but once she heard him say, "Now where in the goddess's name are you?"

"Have we lost something?" she asked, trying not to sound desperate for breath, at which point he stooped down to pick up a herb.

"There you are, chew on this, Ourania, it will give you strength."

"Ah and now we will see the advantage of having a high priest of the earth with us, I hope you will teach me some of your secrets, Bion." Ourania was intrigued as to what knowledge the Lemurians had that differed to the Atlanteans.

"In time, Ourania, in time."

"May I ask what it is?"

"It is a leaf from the Suma root," Bion explained.

Within a short while, she could start to feel the benefits. Ianthe also noticed an increased enthusiasm in Ourania's step, "It seems that Bion has found your energy for you, Priestess," taunted Ianthe.

Bion was quick add to the jibe. "Maybe we can find her something to help with her colour, as well," Bion teased as Ourania's cheeks resembled a red rose, and now they all laughed.

In Atlantis, the tendency was to lean more towards using the crystals alongside with the energy fields and elements but Ourania soon began to feel the benefits of her new-found energy, she began to wonder if Atlanteans would be able to utilize plants as well.

They now walked with a renewed vigour but in relative silence, however there was plenty being discussed more so between Ourania, Hypatia, Maeja and I through our telepathic link.

"I can feel you smiling, Bion," Ourania stated, her senses always alert.

"Tell me, Ourania, are you in contact with your people?"

"I have just re-established contact with the high priestess, and I am constantly connected to my old friend Hypatia, we have established a connection between the four of us at this moment; and what of yourself, Bion, are you connected with earth-mother?"

"Like you I am always connected; I am talking to her right now."

"Good, as I have been informed that there is much to prepare once we reach our destination."

When they did finally reach their journey's end, Bion informed Ourania that it was a special place, the whereabouts of which is only known to some of his most trusted and valued friends.

"This place gives me a direct link to her," he said. "You know her by name; for in the wisdom of your great crystal, you have named Aglaia after her."

"Gaia!" Ourania's heart jumped, even in the time that Ourania had intimately known Hypatia, she had never failed to surprise her.

"Well, in the ancient tongue her name is Demeta, meaning earth-mother, as is the name Gaia," Bion explained.

Chapter Five

Union of Souls

The cavern was magically protected, from the outside there was little to suggest that it even existed. Places such as this had to be kept secret, for there were those who desired to upset the very balance of the world. Ourania was surprised to see that this location had a striking resemblance to the matriarch's chamber. As they approached a dense bush, it parted to reveal a rock face which in turn opened up to reveal the cavern, Bion's home.

"Blessed be," Ourania said, as she gazed around at the cavern, which was illuminated by crystalline strands that lined the walls. "I am humbled to be in your presence earth-mother," she expressed full of joyful emotion, which caused Ianthe to shed a tear.

Showing little emotion, Bion explained: "Now it is time to sleep, for tomorrow our journey begins."

Sleep came easily, helped with another display of the earth-mother's power, as the women lay down, the ceiling of the cavern seemed to disappear, it went transparent, revealing the evening stars, it truly was a splendid sight to see.

By the time the ladies woke, Bion had already gathered fruits, nuts and herbs, presenting them on an earth table on plates of large leaves.

"Earth-mother has prepared these herbs for us," he said. "They will assist us on our journey; for after we have eaten, we will join with earth-mother and the great crystal."

They ate in silence and when they finished they thanked the earth for her nourishment and prepared themselves for what was to be a memorable journey.

Ianthe was not sure that she would be needed; after all,

she was only there to accompany Ourania. "Priestess, I will be waiting for you over there—" but before she could finish her sentence, Bion interjected.

"My sweet child, what makes you less important than I or Ourania? We are all on the same path and we are all an important branch of a single tree. You being here is not by chance, you are in your rightful place," he said. "So yes, you will be a part of this union and that is the will of the creator."

Ourania could not fault his wisdom as Ianthe looked at her, expecting Ourania to tell Bion that it would be fine if she was to just observe.

"You look to me for assistance but I will not tell you otherwise for I know the truth of it. I trust the great crystal and you were chosen from birth to be here, and for the last time, as your ex-high priestess, I am ordering you to call me Ourania."

Just the mention of the great crystal put Ianthe's mind at rest. In the temple, Ianthe and Timo were the guardians of the great crystal, so knew her intimately although communication with her was only reserved for the high priestess, and it was only Ianthe and Timo who were allowed to cleanse her, this was only done in the presence of the high priestess during the completion of the moon's cycle. Ourania prepared herself and strengthened her connection to Hypatia, Maeja and myself. Ianthe meditated and asked for the strength and courage of the great crystal. When Bion could feel that the ladies were ready, Bion blessed the cavern then pronounced. "We, in this space, call upon all who have business here to come forth and be heard. I open this circle of souls to join in union on this blessed morn."

At that moment, the ground began to tremble and the energy began to change in the cavern. They all sat and closed their eyes to allow the circle to form. As they sat in silence they could begin to feel a build-up of energy; intuitively they all knew to relax and give in to the feeling as they exhaled they began to see their bodies – from a heightened position looking down at their physical bodies – sitting around the circle. Then suddenly we appeared as incorporeal forms.

First to appear was Hypatia then me, Maeja, Timo and finally one whom the Atlanteans didn't know; it was Demeta, earth-mother, in the form of a glowing ball of light. Demeta opened this union, "Hallo to all, I am Demeta the soul of this planet, Hypatia and I have asked for this union of souls, for the time has come to pass on what we wish to share with you."

As Demeta was speaking, we could all feel our energies merging. We all felt as if we were one body; one mind and one soul. The beauty and peace that we all felt in this blessed union was truly natural. When the union reached perfection, a picture started to form. A vision of the earth appeared in our minds. We could all suddenly see the threads of time, not only the past, but the future too. As the vision evolved we found ourselves in the future on this planet. It was much like the earth in which we now lived in, however the population of the world had grown, and all were living in dwellings made of natural stone and wood. Some even lived on water in floating townships. They all spoke the same language and had the ability to use telepathy. This was a world where love and peace was accepted and common place, all were happy.

Humans were not the only inhabitants of this planet, for the earth had become an epicentre for beings from other galaxies. It was a place of inspiration, and throughout the ages it had evolved into something spectacular.

An ethos was formed that generated a greater school of knowledge and understanding from a very young age. The young people who were paired with another, would give birth when the body was at its strongest; the young adults would deliver their child when they were in their twenties, they in turn left their child with their parents, and it was left to the grandparents to raise the child. This meant that the young souls had wise teachers, people who had experienced not only all that this world had to offer but also if they wished they could experience other worlds. This opportunity was taken by all souls, grounding the lessons that were taught to them by their grandparents.

Having lived a full life, the parents were now ready to take on the mantel of teacher, if their child brought a little one into the world. This ensured that children had the full benefit of being raised by wise adults, who had experienced life without regret. It was a perfect vision. Because of this way of life, there was no such thing as negativity and all the human traits that make a person want what another has, did not even exist. They all had exactly what they required and they desired nothing more than what they had.

When the vision faded, Hypatia spoke first.

"That was the plan for this world. Sadly, that plan had to be abandoned; the wisdom of our higher souls knew that it could no longer be accomplished."

Demeta took over from Hypatia:

"There are so many different roads in which this world could travel, if we choose not to intervene, what we will do now is show you two of opposite poles. To do so we will use the wisdom of civilisations from other planets, these planets have had the same opportunities as this world now has. We have looked and listened intently to how humans on this world are evolving. Our benefactors can manipulate time and look ahead to where this world will end up, if it is allowed to follow the natural evolution of the planet, as it is now. We will show you how things will be for the inhabitants of this world if we do not intervene, and we will show you how things may become if we take a path that is felt will benefit not only this planet but the space that this planet occupies."

The initial vision that we saw happened in stages; first, we saw the destruction of Lemuria by the hands of the priests and power mongers. They used and manipulated the years of stored knowledge to wage war on less evolved civilisations. They moved across the land like a plague, acquiring what knowledge they could to strengthen themselves. They quickly became the dominant force on the planet, taking on slaves, and killing who they deemed unfit for work. With the passage of time the slaves started to learn through their captors, the very secrets that enslaved them. The slaves revolted causing the collapse of this war machine.

The Atlanteans however, managed to stave off the Lemurians' advance with the aid of the great crystal and a strong will to maintain peace. Due to the turmoil that was surrounding Atlantis, the priestess of the temple formed a new order to keep a watchful eye on the state of the world around them. They had managed to learn about fields of energy and the entire island was protected by this. Passage through the field was possible, but only after the great crystal looked into the refugees' souls to clarify their intentions and desires.

The Atlanteans had evolved on a more peaceful path, they knew that they were well protected and could assist the world if called upon; due to the energy field they had time to further expand their knowledge and wisdom, free from any outside influences. News of the Atlantean resistance to the Lemurian threat soon reached the ears of people fleeing the Lemurian advance, as such Atlantis was seeing a major influx of people seeking shelter. Nevertheless, gradually all the refugees and outsiders that had fled to Atlantis had become disillusioned. They began to ignore the teachings of the Atlanteans and started to follow the path of their homeland, some craved to return to their homelands. Many mourned for their former way of life; Atlantean culture felt foreign to them and although some tried, they never found happiness in this strange land. The outsiders bemoaned the Atlanteans and they started to perceive their once saviours as dictators. Eventually they tried to steal the great crystal using magnetic energy, which caused a powerful imbalance of energy. They thought by using the great crystal's power, they could find a way home and break through the energy field that protected Atlantis. This imbalance damaged the crystal and the entities that placed her here could not help her, they had been instructed to leave the planet to its own fate, this was the will of the creator, to whom they answered without question. It was his command to allow the inhabitants of this world free will, leaving the entities powerless to stop the destruction of the great crystal. The great crystal was overburdened, which caused a chain reaction throughout the planet. This damaged the earth's core beyond repair and the planet was lost.

The second vision saw how the planet would be with the divine intervention of Demeta and Hypatia. Lemuria was lost, followed years later by Atlantis. The great crystal was returned to her keepers but not before seeds of knowledge were implanted into the earth in various forms for man to find. The discovery of this knowledge would only happen when the mistakes of the past were learnt and mastered, and the minds of the inhabitants evolved to a level for the acceptance of love and peace. As a result, the world was then allowed to continue its existence. However, intervention from outside its natural realm would be forbidden. Only during times of great need where the very balance of all realms was at stake, was Demeta allowed to influence the outcome of events.

Eventually humans did evolve but it was only after a lot of pain and suffering. Still, many millennia passed and many a brave soul was sacrificed before the world was ready to be fully realised. People's sense of self-awareness grew and they learned to see their own existence in other ways. They were no longer troubled by what others had that they did not, they no longer quarrelled over differences, all their petty struggles were forgotten. They learned how to live together and live in peace and harmony, respecting the earth and the earth-mother. The visions faded leaving all with a sense of purpose, the nature of this union meant that everyone knew when it was their time to speak.

Bion felt the energy rise in him and was the first to respond.

"Can this course be averted? And is there any hope for my people and Atlantis, or is the lust for power too great?"

Maeja felt the energy shift in her direction and she passed a comment to Bion's statement.

"From what I have witnessed about the human condition, the female of your species has a more loving, gentle approach to living. They are gentle, kind and compassionate, and their instinct is to nurture. They are the gardeners of humanity. The male counterpart has a selfish tendency that points them towards acquisition; they are the hunters, collectors, and their tendency points them towards a more violent path that will consume them with no regards to their fellow human. It is self-destructive in its very nature, given the chance, they will create great pain to achieve what they believe to be their rightful place in this world."

To my surprise, Timo came forward.

"I feel there will be a long road to travel before the hearts of men and women find balance in their masculine and feminine nature. The imbalance that they exhibit will continue until a soul brave enough can teach them the importance of balance and what can be gained by accepting the principle of oneness." I could feel the shift of energy fall on me. The group were awaiting my input.

"I have given this some thought," I said, "and I agree with Maeja. When Lemuria is lost to us the Atlantean people will welcome refugees if there are any, with open arms, but I fear Atlanteans will soon come to exploit Lemurians for their own personal gain, Lemurian people will then look to impose their culture on Atlantis and the acquisition of power will engulf them, and they will have forgotten the sacred bond between man and the earth. When that day comes, Atlantis will be lost."

"The time for half measures must and will cease," Bion said, however now he was more animated. "We who gather here must sow the seeds of knowledge for the future children of the earth."

"We must use the crystals, the sea and the land to

implant this wisdom and knowledge," Ourania interjected. "There will be those who will be gifted with the knowledge and wisdom to access the keys to open the door for humankind, but there will also be humans who will fight the transition and try to suppress this knowledge, for they will fear change. Those who have power will not want to relinquish it, they will not simply hand it over. Instead, they will create situations that will slow down the process, causing terrible pain and suffering to this world; even the wisdom of our teachers cannot stop their need to control."

"In time, humanity must overcome their blindness, they just must," Ianthe said and we could all feel her anguish.

Everyone agreed with the way forward, and all were in total understanding of their roles and the costs. The energy of this union seemed to focus on me again but it was Hypatia who felt that I needed a gentle push.

"Gaia, you're having thoughts for a reason. It's your place to voice your opinion no matter how it seems or feels."

"It's just that it feels so strange to me."

"Have you not stopped to consider that the tree has many branches, who's to say which branch is the correct one that will hold the weight of the future for this world?"

"It's just that what I am seeing is a path that could give salvation to the world and achieve a peaceful end, but I am not steadfast in my conviction," I was nervous but was forced to continue. Hypatia was now more forceful although in my heart I knew that she could see all that I could see.

"Then as part of this union, it is of great importance to share your vision. Gaia, you are now high priestess of the greatest civilization that the world will know for an age. Now you question your ability to use what is your natural talent and gift, and try to hide in the shadows. Gaia, that will not be possible, for you are now in the eye of the hurricane, and it is for you, as well as all here today, to navigate the world out of this situation to a safe harbour. I

45

tell you now, what you see and feel may well be our salvation, so speak your mind, my child, no one here will chastise you for it."

I could feel the pressure and weight. This was my first real test as high priestess. I forced myself to reveal what it was that I saw.

"Well..." I was nervous so started gingerly trying to choose my words carefully. "What I think I saw was a collaboration between the two civilizations, a co-operative mission if you like, where the people of Lemuria and the people of Atlantis were escorted to a place that is best described as a hidden realm underneath the earth. There they will stay until the time is right for their re-entry on to the surface."

Bion was intrigued. "So is this to be for all of the people? How can this be? When we know that there are some in Lemuria who seek to destroy her and... goddess forbid... the planet."

I suddenly felt in control and more confident in my stance.

"No not all, and the same applies for the Atlanteans. Only those who the earth-mother and Hypatia deem fit and worthy to be the guardians of what can be acquired with time, and only those whose hearts are pure and can keep to the principle of oneness may go to the realm beneath the earth."

"Gaia, this is indeed a plan, an exceptional plan," Hypatia said. "However, you all need to see and understand that you as a group are indeed ready to face the many possibilities that lie ahead of you." Hypatia and Demeta were both pleased with this first of many meetings, and it was now time for Hypatia to close the circle.

"This blessed union has come to a close," Hypatia said. "We thank the wisdom of our overseers and our host the earth-mother. We all know what will be expected of us, so until the time comes when we meet again. Blessed be."

They all returned the blessing: "Blessed be."

What followed for Ourania, Bion, Maeja and I was the vision of our final day in clarity, it was a gift from earth-mother and Hypatia.

Chapter Six

Preparation

Maeja woke early the following morning. She was still in pain from an alligator bite she received weeks earlier. Maeja had now established herself a routine where she walked the halls before the order of the light had begun to rise from their chambers. On this particular morning, she turned the corner towards the great central chamber, and nearly bumped into the high priest. This shocked her, as nobody was usually up at this time, and his presence had alarmed her so much that her reaction woke me up.

"What has alarmed you so, Maeja?" I asked.

"Kaius is outside the central chamber and he has shielded himself!"

"Be careful, Maeja," I said. "This is most unfortunate, as he will now know that we will be watching him. Keep him there, I will join you presently."

With that, I woke Timo and together we went to meet with Maeja. Despite this being a serious matter, observing her sitting and not allowing Kaius to move was an amusing sight. I addressed Kaius trying not to show my hand.

"Kaius, it concerns me that you should be outside the chamber at this hour. Your presence here is not in keeping with your station; why do you seek the chamber without my presence at this early point of the day?"

It was common knowledge that any person who wished to seek the advice of the great crystal had to seek approval from the high priestess first, and given that I was now the high priestess, that responsibility would be mine. If their wishes were granted, then they would be allowed to accompany me, knowing that I alone would converse with Hypatia.

"Priestess, I am embarrassed to say that sleep took me

out of my chambers and found me here looking at your pet." Maeja rose on all fours at that blatant slur at her and I had to use force as well as telepathic command to control her temper, for she would have surely caused him harm.

I knew that he was not truthful, nevertheless I played along. "Embarrassing indeed, Kaius, may we escort you back to your chambers?"

"Good Lord, no, priestess. I have embarrassed myself enough, and now that I am back in my true self, I should be fine, apologies, priestess." With that said he was on his way. I sent Maeja to follow him as a precaution; taking no chances Hypatia shielded her, keeping him off her energies in case he had the ability to sense her.

I entered the great chamber with Timo. We stood under Hypatia to check on her energies and then I took Timo to the chamber of the matriarch. When we arrived at the wall, I spoke to Timo: "I have been instructed to bring you here by Hypatia. This chamber is sacred and not known by anyone except Maeja and I. Hypatia has instructed me that our trust for each other will be better served if we bonded. You will not be granted access to this place without Maeja or my presence for now. By us bonding Timo, our paths up to this moment will be shared, we will see all that needs to be seen, and we will be able to communicate telepathically."

Timo looked pleased that Hypatia had spoken of her and trusted her enough to share this space. I took her by the hand and proceeded to walk towards the wall, but Timo held back. "Priestess, there is nothing but wall, so why do you walk so?"

I turned and smiled at her. "Trust and faith, Timo, trust and faith. No harm will come to you." I felt Timo relax so we proceeded. Timo closed her eyes as she followed very tentatively. "Timo," I said. "Open your eyes."

"Oh, Priestess, what is this trickery? We were by a wall and now we are in a chamber, yet we walked but a few steps."

"That Timo will take an age to explain but in time you

49

will come to understand. More importantly, Timo, in this place we are shielded from the likes of Kaius, who wishes to influence our culture for his own betterment. Now we will wait for Maeja, she is also needed for this bonding."

Maeja finally made her entrance through the wall which gave Timo quite a shock.

"I don't think I will ever get used to seeing that, Priestess."

This made us laugh but we had to get on with the bonding, Timo was tentative but calm, I gave Timo time to adjust and when I felt that she was in a more receptive place, I began to explain my bond with Maeja.

"As you know, Maeja and I have a bond and an ability to speak with each other. Hypatia has given you permission to be able to speak to me on that same level. That way, if you or I have concerns that we do not wish for another to hear, we may express ourselves freely through our mind connection. This amulet is connected to my bracelet and it will allow you this gift, which will feel strange at first, so you must practise as much as possible when we have private moments. The headpiece that Maeja wears is also part of the same connection. In time, you may speak with her, providing she permits it of course. This will allow your attention to remain focused on the matter at hand and no one will be any the wiser."

"I understand, but is this not deceitful?" Timo was correct but the situation with Kaius had to be watched with careful eyes.

"That much is true, Timo," I explained. "But it is needed. Do not take off the amulet or reveal its purpose at any time to anyone. Anyone!"

"Yes, Priestess I understand."

"Now, what follows will have you uneasy for we will blend our souls, this will allow the link. I will see images of your birth in a flash. My first experience was gentle for me, as I had been prepared for it during my childhood, through visions and energy transference from the great crystal and Hermione. Now, sit beside Maeja, she will give you the strength you will need through this energy transference. When I place this around your neck, the process will begin."

Timo sat and signalled that she was ready. I placed the amulet on Timo and was guided through her life thus far. Everything was as expected, all but two facts: first, Timo and Ianthe were sisters, which I felt I should have known. They were born to a family that had no ties to the temple, they lived out in the fields amongst the animal kingdom. Their parents cared and treated animals, and were well known by humans and animals alike. Timo and Ianthe were brought to the temple by their parents when they were only children. Only Hypatia and Hermione were aware what part they would play in the future, and they would personally train the two girls to put them on the path that they were now on. The second surprise from the bonding was that both Timo and Ianthe had the ability to telecommunicate with the animal kingdom. This was a natural gift from birth; however, one that they had been unaware of and a talent that would not develop until much later in life when and if they followed in the family tradition, this was the way it always was for their family lineage.

When the process was complete, Timo wept with joy, feeling as close to me as she did to her sister, she too saw my life unfold. We sat for a while to allow her time to get used to the feeling and then practised a little. As expected Timo took to it instantly. We left the chamber and walked in the gardens for a time, talking telepathically when no one was present; it would prove to be an invaluable tool in the years to come.

Although Ourania had warned me about Kaius, I felt that my early days as high priestess was better served strengthening my link with Hypatia. I had learnt to trust my intuition and allowed that to guide me, but now my intuition was telling me that Kaius needed constant monitoring, a task that Maeja and Timo would come to enjoy, through it they would become very close friends with a bond as strong as mine. Hypatia had instructed us how to shield our thoughts and to protect ourselves from Kaius as he was becoming more persistent, she also allowed us to make our own mistakes from time to time. Hypatia wanted us to experience all that temple life had to offer as well as the complexities of the human condition. She wanted us to see this through our own eyes, which was to say that she would not interfere unless we requested her to do so.

When I questioned her on this one day her reply was simply to say, "You are a free spirit… and that's the way we want you to be." I had the impression that she was ever watching me to see what direction I would choose to walk.

In the night, I had heard from Ourania in my sleep, and I wanted to talk to her about Kaius. Ourania had reached the land of the Lemurians. When I woke up, Maeja was sitting by my bed. I smiled at her and then we went to the matriarch's chamber, which we liked to refer to as M's place. When we arrived, we sat in the centre of the room and established the link with Ourania, I could sense that she was having to rush. "Is all well, Ourania?" I asked.

"Yes, Gaia, but it seems that Bion is in a hurry to get to where he is going… an act that I am not accustomed to."

"And let's not forget your age," I said.

"Oh, I see Hypatia has allowed you to keep your childish humour."

"Yes, she has," I said, but now I could feel that Ourania was having difficulty. "What is troubling you, Ourania?"

"Bion has given me a herb to help with my – as you call it – old age, and it tastes putrid."

I was still in my teens. Ianthe and Timo were both in their early thirties, and Ourania was well into her middle eighties… and Bion was even older. Longevity was part of the gift bestowed to high priests and priestesses, which was a good thing as it was not usual to achieve high priestess status until later on in life. Ourania, however, had achieved her status by the age of forty-six, which was a huge accomplishment.

"Oh my," Ourania said. "It seems to be working. Perhaps you can learn to incorporate herbs in your healings. Ask Hypatia to assist you in strengthening our link so you don't miss opportunities."

"Maybe you would have me bathe the priestesses each morning too," I said.

Maeja laughed. "Hallo, Maeja," Ourania said. "I see the new priestess is a bit touchy and lazy too… you must whip her in shape for me."

"Oh, you will never know it is hard keeping order here in your absence, Gaia needs so much attention."

"Maeja, you disloyal mouse," I said jokingly.

"Gaia, I feel that you want to discuss Kaius."

"OK, back to serious matters it is then," Maeja then rested her head in my lap as we talked.

"He was found outside the central chamber early one morning. I know he was up to bad things, and it seems that he is getting desperate."

"Yes, we were aware that he would try to manipulate Hypatia. Have you established a telepathic link with Hypatia yet?"

"Yes, I have also joined with Timo."

"Good, all is moving as planned, through your connections jointly you will be able to keep him at bay for the time being."

"For the time being! That does not sit well with me."

"Do not worry; there is much to do and Hypatia is wise she will not let you stumble; Gaia, all is where it should be."

I could sense Hypatia needed us so we said our farewells, and I linked in with Hypatia.

"You must come to the central chamber to prepare for a joining and call on Timo."

We all arrived at the chamber together. Hypatia spoke to me and I relayed the information to Timo:

"Hypatia tells me that we all must meditate and draw on the power of all her brothers and sisters, we have an important joining in the later hours." This is all I was told.

Maeja did not protest, and Timo trusted Hypatia. During the time that we spent in the chamber meditating, the head priestess instructed the priestesses to occasionally look in on us, however, they did not disturb us as respect was always given to those who were in meditations.

As we meditated, we could sense the power of all the crystals. With it we could feel our bodies getting lighter and our temperature rising. Telepathically, Hypatia spoke through me for Timo to hear and understand. "My children, your consciousness will be transported across the vast ocean, we will be joining with Ourania and Ianthe the high priest of Lemuria and a special guest."

I was very excited; this for all of us was a new experience. I could instantly feel that Timo was nervous about what Hypatia had explained but she put her trust in all that she had come to know and see in her time at the temple. In that moment I began to see that this lady had a lot of inner strength and now I was beginning to see why it was that she was put on my path.

In the central chamber, the priestesses had grown concerned that we had been there for so long, we had been sat in meditation for over half of the day; when the time had arrived for us to link in with our friends across the water, Hypatia started glowing and pulsating. The priestesses knew at that moment it was time to leave the room but to stay close. As they left the chamber, Claritia remained behind. She had taken over from Ianthe and in such cases, only Timo and Claritia would be permitted to stay, and as Timo had to spend more time with me, the task of caring and cleaning Hypatia had become a solitary role. When all the priestesses cleared the chamber Hypatia closed and sealed the doors, all the priestesses without exception sat down in meditation. It was then that Hypatia began to change, it was an event that had never been witnessed by any past and present who served at the temple.

A cloud started forming from the crystal, which materialised into the figure of a woman – it was Hypatia.

Hypatia sat with us to form a circle, we did not open our eyes or lose concentration but we all could feel her presence, then the crystal emanated a glowing dome of light. This dome encased the circle and all Claritia could do was watch patiently. News of the doors sealing spread around the temple and it was not long before it reached the high priest.

Kaius was in his chambers when his most trusted priest and conspirator, Macedon, came running in looking extremely flustered. Kaius was vexed at this rude interruption:

"What is so important that you would dare enter my chambers in such a disrespectful manner? If I was not high priest, I would have you flogged to make an example of you."

"My apologies, high priest, but the central chamber has sealed."

"And for this you rush in here like an ant looking for food! The chamber seals all the time."

"Yes, this is true, but not with the high priestess, her pet, and two others inside!"

Now he was intrigued and without a moment's hesitation, he went to the chamber in a manner that was not fitting to his station. On his arrival, the head of the order of priestesses, Chrysanta, stopped her meditation to greet him, as he was demanding to know what was going on.

"It is as it seems, high priest."

Chrysanta did not have much time for Kaius. In her words, *"he is an over achiever and not the ideal person for the responsibility of high priest."* They would often have crossed words.

"The doors are sealed and the high priestess is in conference with the great crystal, anything beyond that is for the high priestess and whomever she has allowed this audience with. You have and will never have the authority to question it."

"How dare you! I am the high priest!" His voice was

raised as Chrysanta's response had provoked him.

"Of the keeper of records," she interjected, "we are of the light. You are not and will never be my master!"

He knew he had crossed the line but he could not back down; after all, he was above her and had worked long and hard to attain his position. At the raising of voices, the priestesses rose from their meditation and joined Chrysanta.

Kaius's cheeks were red with rage: "The high priestess will hear of your insolence," he said.

"As she will yours, now I suggest you leave these halls as you have no business here."

Kaius's thoughts were awash. *Had Gaia discovered his secret? What was the purpose for this meeting?* So many questions and no answers; he would have to be more careful.

On arrival to his chambers, he summoned Macedon: "Gather the shroud," he demanded, something had to be done about this new priestess and soon.

After what seemed like an eternity, the doors unlocked and the priestesses entered the chamber. Maeja, Timo and I were still sitting, while Claritia stood between us and the doors. All the priestesses walked to what was their designated places, held up their arms and blessed the room. They then turned to leave in twos with Maeja, Timo and myself in the middle, we made our way to the bathing chamber to be washed.

After we had rested, we went to M's chamber so that we could discuss what we had just learned and what it meant for us, but more importantly, what the connection was between the Lemurians and the high priest Kaius. Hypatia linked in to guide us in the right direction. In her mind, if we kept faith in each other and stayed connected to her, then that was all she could wish for. By the end of our discussion, we agreed to keep watching Kaius and increase the connection to Lemuria via the partnerships between Ourania and myself.

Timo stayed in my chambers for the following week,

and she appeared to be handling the whole situation extremely well, eventually she would be moved to the chamber adjacent to mine, which was seen to be more beneficial for all concerned. Maeja and I believed that her acceptance of all that was happening was purely down to the relationship she had with Hypatia when she was her carer, plus the bond between her and her sister Ianthe.

The temple duties that I felt I needed to attend to were things that the priestesses took care of, but I made a point of overseeing most ceremonies as I felt it was my responsibility to know all there was to know about my children. The head priestess, Chrysanta, insisted that I did not have to attend so many. She often joked about it, but she did have full understanding of why I found it necessary. She also found it comforting knowing that the high priestess was invested in her role, and took a personal interest in the priestesses.

One morning, after tending to a bathing ceremony for a troubled infant, I was taking a stroll in the gardens. I had begun to take little strolls alone against the wishes of Maeja and Timo. "You risk too much," Maeja would stress.

"I have you, Timo and Hypatia to keep me safe," would be my usual reply.

In a quiet part of the garden, a voice called for me, which I instantly recognised. "Stay close, my friend." I linked in with Maeja as there was something about his energy that gave me a foreboding.

"I already am," Maeja would never let me stray too far on my own if Kaius was on the temple grounds.

"Gaia," Kaius called again, however, this time trying to sound more authoritative.

Maeja was amused but concerned: "Why do you tease him so?"

"He will address me with respect or not at all."

Kaius now drew closer as did Maeja, who had the element of stealth. She positioned herself close enough to protect me if he became a clear threat to my wellbeing.

"Gaia, I call to you but you pay me no mind. Have you difficulty in knowing your own name?"

"To you high priest, I am high priestess, as I am to all who know me. I have afforded you the respect of your position and you will please afford me the respect and do the same."

"How dare you!" The rage was coursing through his veins, and before he could continue, Maeja pounced out from behind a bush to stand between us both, an act that made the high priest's heart start racing.

"Now, am I to believe that you wish to discuss a matter with me?" I asked calmly.

He took a moment to consider my words: "Gaia, you may have your pet to protect you, but make no mistake, you antagonise the wrong priest. I am not one of your children, as you like to call them. I am Kaius, high priest of the temple."

I turned to Maeja, stroked her head, petted her ears and bent down to her. "Aw, my sweet pet, don't be upset, the mean man is just a little shocked that you were there to protect me against danger. He would never have raised his voice if he knew you were there."

Maeja wanted to laugh; instead, she calmly linked in keeping a close eye on Kaius and said, "Had he have raised his hand that would have been my lunch sorted."

"Maeja, how could you?" now in both their minds they laughed.

Now Kaius was raging. "You mock me, child."

I now stood and turned calmly to face him and looked deep in to his eyes.

"As I have said, you will address me as high priestess, a position that was gifted to me from Hypatia and Ourania, the high priestess and the great crystal of Atlantis. If, however, you have a problem with the wisdom and judgement of powers higher than your own, you are more than welcome to take it up with the grandmaster, who will consult with me as high priestess. In turn, I will consult with the order of light and then with Hypatia. Following that, I will inform the grandmaster of the decision, who will then inform you. And just to be clear, as I am sure you are aware, I have the power to remove you from the position of high priest; however, you do not and will never have the authority to remove me from my post. Now, if you wish to continue to test my ability, strength and resolve as high priestess, I can assure you it is a battle that you will lose. So, if your business here is indeed important, then may I suggest that you come to the council chamber at the appropriate time and put your petition forward in the correct manner, for this is my time for my meditation."

Before he could respond, Maeja walked forward to let him know that his impromptu meeting was over. Kaius had no option but to turn tail and lick his wounds.

"Oh, Maeja, that felt so good."

"Gaia," Hypatia spoke to me, as she was always connected to the three of us. "I am impressed with your composure and strength. You have developed much faster than we had hoped for. Ourania will be pleased at your resolve. We always had total faith in you and belief that you are the correct candidate for what is to come… and now Kaius knows it too."

The praise that came from Hypatia was so full of love that I felt tears rolling down my cheeks. Maeja rubbed up on my leg and we both sat and closed our eyes to meditate on what just happened with Kaius. It was not surprising to see visions of Kaius walking in dark corners talking to people whose faces were shielded. However, what was seen in this vision was the fact that his life was in danger; in fact, it was going to be cut short. This left me with the question: *Do I warn him of his pending fate or do I allow his path to unfold in the direction in which it is going?* A thought that Hypatia was quick to answer.

"My sweet child, Kaius's path is his and his alone. If you intercede, it will merge you with his path, this will interrupt yours and bring you into his circle, putting you in the position of sharing his fate. Such is the strength of his ill doing, you have been given this vision only to show you how destructive negativity is to humans who lust for power over love. Use this as a lesson to help you with decisions that you must make."

This warning came as a stern reminder that I was to be the last high priestess.

***

Six years had passed when I felt my first burst of uncomfortable energy. On one of my walks that I liked to take when not performing my tasks and duties, I rounded a corner to see a man talking to one of Kaius's priests. I had never seen this man before but the energy that was emanating from him was tainted; it felt dirty, impure. I sent out a message to Maeja: "Maeja, come quickly, something is not good here."

"Yes I know. I am between you and them to your right."

Unlike myself, Maeja had become somewhat of an expert when it came to shielding herself, something she practised often while out hunting. She followed me on most days that I went for my walks.

As I drew closer to the men, the stranger turned rather quickly and then left in the opposite direction.

"I have seen you with Kaius on several occasions haven't I," I said. "If I am not mistaken, your name is Macedon."

"Yes, it is, High Priestess, and yes, I serve the high priest."

"That man is not of the temple, was he in need of assistance?"

"No, Priestess, this man does work for us from time to time." We both knew this was not truthful. "Maeja, follow him," I said.

"As you wish."

"But be careful, his energy is not good."

"Yes, I felt that too… perhaps there is more to this and

I feel it is connected to Kaius."

Hypatia was also watching. "I was keeping watch over you and I took the liberty of linking in to them. They were indeed discussing Kaius, but they were conspiring to do him harm. Their aim is to put somebody in his position that they can control. They are trying to manipulate our position, Gaia, and the time is fast approaching."

"I understand; I will let Ourania know what is happening here."

"She is in a position where she knows what is happening at all times."

"At all times... Is that not a strain on her with what she has to do in Lemuria?"

"It can be, but I am keeping her fed with information, which I am managing to a level that I know she can handle. But more importantly, Ourania is a very strong lady, so don't let her maturity fool you."

Chapter Seven

The Shroud

The shroud was an underground order formed by a group of men known as the elders. Its goal was for the acquisition of power and knowledge; its purpose was to overthrow the temple, take control of the great crystal and then eventually take control over the inhabitants of the world. The order operated in darkness using the negative side of energy; as for the identity of its founders, it has been a closely guarded secret that even Kaius was not privy to.

The walk to the gathering place was full of twists and turns. It was a cave that ran deep into the earth and with a lot of work by the elders, it provided protection from the great crystal. It was set in a cove on the shoreline, which was as secret as it was difficult to get to. The shroud consisted of forty members from all crafts and walks of life. Although Kaius was high priest and very ambitious, he was not the leader of the shroud. He was recruited when the shroud was in its infancy, and in his role as high priest it had been noted how impatient he had become. Furthermore, he was displeased with his position and level of responsibility within the temple.

The shroud had tolerated his arrogant behaviour as it served a purpose and kept the focus on him rather than the elders. The meeting that Kaius called for years earlier did not sit well with the elders, when the meeting began Kaius was very elevated when he addressed the members of the shroud. Kaius went to great lengths to explain what he had just witnessed, while choosing to leave out his embarrassment at the hand of the head priestess. The true leader of the shroud was groomed from childhood by the real powerbase of the shroud, he was a man that was quick to temper, and was highly skilled in the art of using negative energy. Finally, he had heard enough and let his presence be known up to that point under instruction from the elders he had kept a low profile, his voice came bellowing out from the crowd.

"This is the reason why you have summoned the shroud with no warning, preparation or blessing from the elders." His voice was loud and there could be no mistake as to the level of his anger, the members around him parted, to reveal the lord who made his way to Kaius still bellowing his dis-pleasure. "You have put the order in jeopardy. You sense that there could be danger for us, yet you blindly call this gathering, hoping that we would not see through your childish tantrum to seek some sort of revenge for your constant belittlement at the hands of the temple." It was clear that the lord was not best pleased.

"You are proving to be a blemish on what we have established here, a blemish that will not be tolerated for much longer. Kaius, we have allowed you the mantle as lead speaker only. You are not the leader, know your place Kaius." The lord was now face-to-face with Kaius.

"Until the elders can establish what damage has been done here, the shroud will not convene until any and all threats to our survival can be verified."

All who were present knew not to question his word for to do so would mean death. One man did question his word once and his life ended that night in his sleep. The lord was trained in how to manipulate the body to induce illness, making the cause of death look like a natural occurrence. Once again, Kaius had overstepped, however, this time he feared for his life.

The members left the cave leaving just Kaius and the lord, "Kaius, your wish to be higher than you are is a quality that will cause you great harm. We will not allow your ambition to affect our order, do you understand what I am telling you?"

Kaius said nothing, but the silence was telling enough for the lord.

"Keep yourself quiet, Kaius. Live in the shadows that is

our way, let what you seek come to you and stop chasing what does not wish to be caught, this is as much of a warning as it is advice; the elders are very concerned with your persistence in pushing for more power. This is the only time I will speak of this." The lord had spoken and there would be no second chances.

Macedon had seen enough as a member to know that if Kaius was spoken to alone, he was either dead or being watched by the lord. Either way, the outcome would not be good for Kaius. Macedon had decided that he had to safeguard his own life, so prepared to ensure his survival. He had sent word out that he needed a meeting with the lord and within three days, a messenger came to see him. "The lord has guaranteed your safety; he is aware that you are innocent. However, the elders need eyes and therefore he has called upon your services."

Macedon knew what was being asked of him. Being Kaius's co-conspirator in the temple meant that this was going to be a difficult task, but Macedon feared the lord more than he feared the high priest. Nevertheless, he was smart enough to know that if he played his hand correctly, he would be looked upon favourably.

Kaius knew that the shroud would be watching him and was certain that they would approach Macedon to keep them informed. It was a cat and mouse game that each participant played very well.

Over a long period of time Kaius was noticing his loss of connectional strength to the temple, so much so, he was now getting more irrational in his dealings with me. In his mind, I was young and inexperienced, which made him believe that I would be easy to manipulate. He was later to discover that that would not be the case. The following years would teach him to trust the knowledge, wisdom and power of a seasoned ex-high priestess and the power of the crystal.

His arrogance would be his undoing.

Chapter Eight

Lemuria

Over the years that passed in Lemuria, Ourania and Ianthe had plenty to discuss with Bion, even more so after the joining of souls. Ourania's mind was racing with questions; she didn't know where to start and she felt like a child who had their first telepathic experience with their animal. "Wow, Hypatia told me to be prepared for some things that were going to widen my knowledge, but that was incredible." Ourania's' excitement filled the cavern. "I have had similar experiences with some of my initiates, but to have a full-blown joining of souls… well, that was a truly amazing experience."

That was her initial reaction after the first joining, to which Bion let out a full and jolly laugh which did not sway Ourania. "But my first question is about the herbs and my thoughts about using them in conjunction with the crystals to help people. Please tell me more about the herbs."

"There is much to learn, Ourania," Bion said. "I have been studying these herbs for my entire priesthood."

"I am a quick study," Ourania said.

"I thought you were going to say that. Well, I have been guided to or I should say instructed through visions to make a record of what I have learned."

"I see," Ourania said. "Well, I guess Hypatia and Gaia have been busy in their preparations."

Now they both laughed. Ianthe made herself busy cleaning the cavern whilst Ourania and Bion poured over the pages of his studies. Her studies lasted for a number or years, and as stated she was an exceptional student.

For a cave dwelling, it was remarkably easy to keep clean. Nearby was a stream that led to a small lake with a gentle flowing waterfall, which was to become an extremely revitalising place to wash and meditate, the beauty of this place could not compare, Ianthe would often wonder if it was through Demeta's intervention that helped keep this place looking so perfect and have a peaceful presence about it, a question that in time she put to Bion.

Bion was more than happy to explain to the women: "This place sits on one of Demeta's many power lines that provide vital energy to all that honour her. This power line comes directly from her heart centre and she has gifted this to us to aid us in the years to come. It is pure energy and keeps our location highly protected from those who seek to find me, which number many. When we leave this place, she will draw it back into her heart as it is only here for our use and protection."

The pages that Bion wrote were extremely helpful and the applications of the healing plants alongside the crystals would be very beneficial to so many. Ourania felt a slight tinge of sorrow in her heart as she read, and she thought what good could be accomplished if there was more time to digest and put into practice a guided regimen of cures. Nevertheless, she knew that the plan was made and nothing could change that.

Bion made himself busy, whilst Ourania continued to read it took her many years to read through what was written and even then, the digestion of the pages would take her years to fully comprehend, time that she knew she did not have.

One morning after the first meal was consumed, Bion left the ladies to go out into the forest; when he was finished gathering some herbs and plants, he called both women over. "Now, what I have gathered up here is a collection of plants that are going to help us enter the heart of Lemuria unnoticed. It is important that you study and remember what I am doing here, for it will become invaluable to you both, your energy is more refined and vibrates at a higher frequency to ours. When the mixture is ready, you must drink it all, and by the time we reach Lemuria, your energy will take on a Lemurian format.

Once there we will go to meet with some loyal friends, they are aware of my mission, and they have been helping me keep safe and out of danger."

***

The walk to Lemuria was a long one that took three weeks to complete. On their journey, they talked of many things and I was very prominent in their discussions. They cleared the forest to be met by a wall circling the city, this was alien for Ourania and Ianthe as there was no need for such a structure in Atlantis.

"Why does this place have such a structure surrounding it?" Ourania felt uncomfortable. *Is the Lemuria plight that severe?* she wondered.

"Due to the nature of how our people have become so immersed in the acquisition of power, it has caused a separation of the people and their relationship to the earth. Those that have power want more and will even steal to acquire it; those who have little will do unspeakable things to keep it, and those that have their power stolen, will do even worse to get it back. This is the nature of what Lemuria has become, which is why you must be shielded when you are here. Some people can see the energy that we omit, and as ours is of a nature that is so pure and strong, I fear what would happen if we were not prepared. The surrounding wall has been a part of Lemuria for many years now, which is a direct result of the decay that has swallowed our city. Follow me and be mindful of your thoughts," Bion instructed.

Ourania was a little concerned of what she was wearing; in Atlantis there was no need for secrecy, so the covering of heads was not necessary. Therefore, when Bion asked them to put on their cloaks just prior to entering the city, it created a sense of concern. However, on entering the gates of Lemuria it soon became apparent that they would have stood out had they not have done so. It seemed the covering of the head was a common practice and almost an expected thing to do.

On entering the main area of the city, Ourania could feel the energy, which felt so thick it was almost sickening. Bion had already warned them not to show any signs of surprise, compassion, fear or emotion, as it would surely mark them as outsiders. They had to blend in if their protection was to hold true.

They soon left the main street and started making their way down side alleys, where the energy seemed to get thicker with every street they turned down. The way that people were treating each other was unpleasant and something that Ourania could not even begin to describe. Bion was beginning to see in the women a sense of empathy and was now very concerned for the women, so much so that he had to find a quiet corner and pull them aside. "Ladies, be careful lest your thoughts betray you. I fear better preparation was needed, can you compose yourselves?"

"We will try," was all that they could say with tears in their eyes.

Bion chose his route with more care; trying to avoid contact with the locals, he knew that some of the worst areas of Lemuria could not be avoided but his destination had to be reached. With the attention that was given to his capture, his meetings in the city had to be conducted in places that a person such as he would not usually be seen in.

"We have arrived," Bion announced and not a moment too soon. When the women went through the doors, they could not contain themselves any longer. Ianthe released the pain that she was so desperately trying to contain. Ourania could draw on her experience as high priestess to stave the feelings of great sorrow, for what was once a great civilisation.

"Ladies, I feel that I must apologise for not preparing you better," Bion said, "but you needed to see what we were dealing with for our mission to succeed. However, I have brought herbs that will help you with the realisation of what you have just witnessed, and replenish your protection."

Bion introduced the women to four men. The most prominent and most trusted was a man called Petrus. Bion had explained before they left for the city that Petrus had never had any affiliation to their temple or priest structure. Bion and Petrus were brought together by a set of visions that ensured that their first meeting was held in total secrecy and that no person linked to the temple knew of their meetings.

The first couple of meetings were more about fact-finding and the building of trust, and once this was established, the real work began.

"Hi, Petrus," Bion said. "I am happy to find you well, my friend. This is Ourania and Ianthe."

"I see the journey here has put a great strain on them," Petrus said, instantly seeing the energy fluctuations in both women, but more so in Ianthe. Petrus held out his hand, "Please take my hand I will assist you. We must learn to control your energy or else all will be in danger." Petrus could tell by the look on Ianthe's face that she was at the early stage of passing out. He brought her over to a stool in the far corner of the room. "Please sit, Ianthe, is it? If you please, I am going to guide through a mental exercise to help you to control your energy. We in Lemuria call it our chi; it is our life force energy that connects us to the earth-mother." Petrus had grown to be a very powerful conduit in the time that he and Bion had spent together. His vision and ability was a purely natural development, which came about due to his integrity and love for mankind.

"Now, Ianthe, I want you to picture a glowing light that surrounds your body." Although Ianthe knew what Petrus was describing, she knew that this was a voyage of discovery and learning so did not interrupt.

"Good, that's it."

Ourania was watching from the other side of the room, listening intently. "What is he seeing, Bion?" she asked. "How does he know what she is doing?"

"Petrus can see energy clearly and as he is talking to her, he is seeing her energy shrink and become covert to other Lemurians."

"Can you see this too?" she asked, keeping her attention firmly on Ianthe and Petrus.

"Yes I can."

Ourania could feel the humour in his voice so now she turned to face Bion: "So, how is my energy?" Observing the look of joy on his face as she asked: "Is it something I said?"

"Actually, it is something you did. As Petrus was talking to Ianthe, your energy began to shrink also. Although I must say, yours was not as bad as Ianthe's but Petrus is a very gifted soul. He knew who needed the most assistance and who was the strongest."

Petrus had finished with Ianthe and had instructed her to sit while he joined Bion and Ourania. "Please accept my apologies," he said. "I see as expected that you have managed to draw in your energy."

"What do you mean as expected?"

"Your energy field is different from Ianthe's, it's stronger, which I suspect is because of where you are from. Are you involved with working with the elements?"

"Not exactly, I work with crystals and they are the focal point of my knowledge."

"Mmm, Bion did inform me to expect visitors from afar whose knowledge and gifts have an important role to play in the times ahead of us. May I ask what distant shores you hail from?"

"We are from—"

Before she could finish her sentence, Bion interjected: "Far away. That is all that is needed to be said for now."

Petrus revealed a side of himself that not too many people were aware of. He linked in with Ourania telepathically.

"Please control your face and energies, as only Bion and my brothers know I share this gift." He was testing her strength for the other three men were in fact his brothers.

Ourania was surprised but managed to stay composed, while Petrus continued: "I know where it is that you are from. You are Atlantean and a high priestess and I am truly honoured to be in your presence."

"As I am yours," Ourania said. "But, Petrus, you try to deceive me as these men are your brothers."

Petrus smiled a smile of acknowledgement. "Yes, but I had to know how evolved you are. Please forgive my deception, but these are troubled times as you are aware." Petrus then continued the conversation verbally. "Well, can you at least enlighten me as to why there was such an energy imbalance in you ladies?"

"We do not suffer the torment that we have just witnessed whilst walking through your streets… this was a hard and shocking sight to see."

Ianthe was feeling a lot better now and joined Ourania, Bion and Petrus. "Thank you, Petrus. I will remember that exercise for I am sure I will need it again." Now Bion was eager to conduct the business that they had come for, as spending too much time in the city was not healthy for him or his party.

They all joined the other men who were sitting at a table with fresh fruits and nuts to eat, and they discussed the order of business whilst they were eating. Bion learned that the priest who had overturned him had learned that he was in the forest and that he was being helped by the earth-mother. He long suspected that Bion was getting help to stay so elusive and that it was somebody outside of the temple. In his bid to find Bion, many of Bion's closest friends in the temple were tortured for information, but with no results, as it seemed that Bion was always one step ahead of him.

After what seemed like a short time, Bion concluded his business and informed the women that it was time to leave. He turned to Petrus and asked if he would help Ianthe to prepare herself and he would work on Ourania. The other three men went outside to keep a watchful eye on the streets. Ourania had noticed that in the meeting they did not say a word, something that Ianthe also found peculiar and she questioned this matter to Petrus. "Why is it that your brothers do not speak?"

"Their tongues were removed by the priest who is known as the butcher. We have found other ways of communicating, which in fact is better for us and serves us well."

The brothers were waiting for them when they stepped outside, and they nodded to acknowledge that all was safe. Ianthe felt confident now that she was better prepared for the walk to the city gates, and knowing that Petrus was by her side, seemed to give her added strength. To her surprise, she found that she was attracted to him. Ourania was walking with Bion, while two of the brothers walked ahead, the others followed behind, and the last took the rear at a short distance. They could all see the gates just ahead, but to Ourania's surprise, the brothers changed direction.

"What seems to be the problem?" Ourania asked. "I can see the gates, so why do we not walk to them? Is there something you wish us to see?"

"Ourania, these men have abilities that surpass my own," Bion said. "I have learnt to trust them with my life. I do not ask, I only know to follow, and as such I have stayed out of harm's way."

The gift that the four brothers shared was not exclusive to Petrus's family. In Lemuria, Bion had stated that it was not unusual for people to see energy, and this was one of the tools used by the priest to capture any would-be rivals for his position. "In his rise to attain power, the mad priest sought out several gifted children. Some were too weak-minded to say no; as they became older, they became his spies and hunters. Those that refused had terrible things done to them to sway their minds. All kind of techniques were used, from torture to brain manipulation; some survived, while others were less fortunate. Petrus's brothers were some of the fortunate ones... fortunate in the loosest of terms, as they had their tongues removed and collected a wide range of scars for their defiance."

"This priest is not a nice man," was all that Ourania could bring herself to say.

Now their procession stopped and waited. It was a dark passageway with a clear view of the gates. Petrus placed a cloak of darkness on Ianthe as soon as he was aware that trouble was ahead. As they waited, Ourania took Bion's advice, closed her eyes and drew in her energy then dimmed it a little.

"Perfect, Ourania, you look like a native of these shores now," Bion jested. No sooner had he spoken when armed troops passed in front of the passageway with two priests and a well-dressed man in between them.

"What is this I am seeing?" Ourania asked, "And why is there a priest with them, and who is that man?"

"This is the very thing that I was afraid of," Bion replied. "The priests have formed an allegiance with an outside force. The mad priest has extended his reach beyond the city; as for the man, I am not sure yet but his energy is not from Lemuria. This is now the way of Lemuria, Ourania. The way of living peacefully has ended. Now, we are dominated by greed and control, ruled by fear. Those men enforce the will of the mad priest. You will please excuse me for I will never use the word high priest."

"I was wondering, but it is understandable," Bion continued. "He has visited other lands and seen how much can be gained with fear, manipulation and intimidation. I should say ascertained or collected but to rule over people is his drive and passion. This has tainted our city. He believes it has made it strong; I, however, know it has made it weak." Ourania could sense that Bion was not happy with what the city had become.

The guards had gone and the brothers continued to the gates. To Ourania's surprise, they walked with them all the way to the cave. At that point, it became apparent to Ourania that these men were trusted with the location of the cavern. He must have trusted them very much and the women would soon learn to trust them too; it was becoming clear to Ourania, that they were to become an integral part of the preparation towards Ourania's final days on earth.

Chapter Nine

The Brothers

Petrus was a stout man, well-educated and well versed in the roles and duties of priesthood. His friends, which he kept to a minimum, had stated that based on his integrity, he would have made a fine city official. They would often question him on his views, to which his answer was always voiced on the side of caution. His true views were brought about by lessons learnt after the troubles that his brothers had felt at the hand of the mad priest. His father was a fisherman, who was not tainted by the lust for power and brought up his family in the old ways. As a result, Petrus was more than concerned at what he was witnessing in how the city was changing for the worst. As he put it, "Things are spiralling out of control and there surely can be only one way that this will end."

His observations served him well. He was not an outspoken kind of man and because of his cautionary ways, Demeta and Hypatia had noticed him. The time came for them to act, and the only course of action for them to take was for them to recruit him to work with Bion. Bion was well versed in communications with Demeta, he had not been introduced to Ourania yet, that was set to happen once Bion had established a tight bond with Petrus. As for Petrus, he was not familiar with either Demeta or the way she worked. It took a long time for Petrus to trust what he was seeing and hearing, Demeta had to be careful not to push him too quickly or too far. Petrus had almost reached the point where he questioned his own sanity. When the time eventually came for these two men to meet, to Petrus's surprise, the person with whom he was going to meet was as pictured in his visions, this made the building of trust an easier task to accomplish. However; Petrus, by nature, made certain that he took plenty of time to get to feel this stranger's energy was of the kind that commanded respect and trust.

"Good evening, Petrus, I am Bion. If I have got my timings correct, you are not here by chance."

"To be honest, I am not sure why I am here," Petrus cautious as always replied with a constant eye on the door but continued. "I have had feelings and dreams to be here this night to meet you, but I have never seen you or even know who you are, much less know what I am doing here. Maybe this is a mistake, but my curiosity took over my instinct to be careful." A needed omission by Petrus.

"That is a good quality to have in these times, Petrus, for it is that very quality that brings me to you now."

"Well, you know my name; however, I don't know who you are. Furthermore, I'm not sure that I belong here." Yet another omission.

"Petrus, you have taken the first step, but if you feel that way then now is the time to make your decision, for our time in this meeting is short."

"Say what you have to say, priest," the words came out without thinking. *Let's see how he uses this,* Petrus thought.

"I will use it to try and persuade you that your time will not be wasted. Yes, Petrus, I can hear your thoughts, as I know you can see my energy in detail. Your thoughts and perceptions are true, and trust that I have respect for you on what I have learned in the short time that we have been here. You know by now that I have been brought here to form an alliance with you. You should also know that I have a special bond with an elemental that is connected to all on this world."

"Let me stop you there," Petrus said. "Yes, it is true that I have concerns for this world and I have picked up that you care for it deeply, but you also are the high priest of the temple, as such the element that you speak of is the earth soul, I have heard of this bond that is shared by the temple and the earth. Yes it can be said the we have learned a lot about each other but how does this concern me?"

"The earth soul that you speak of is known to us as the earth-mother, and she can see things that we cannot. She can see into people's souls as she did with you and she knows that you are an important player in the years to come but also and more importantly your heart is pure. She has guided you here for this meeting so we can help those who want our help. There is much to tell you of her plans but for now just know that you are needed."

"Thus far my life has been simple and that's how I like it," Petrus said. "I have my reasons."

"Your brothers?"

"Yes, my brothers. Do you not think my family have suffered enough at the hands of the temple?" Petrus said with a high level of agitation in his voice.

"We will all have to make sacrifices in the years to come... some more than others, as for those poor souls that have suffered, that is not of my doing." Bion could feel that he needed to tread carefully.

"Are you not the high priest of the temple," Petrus did not try to hide his emotions. "Are you not responsible for the work that your temple and priest do."

"I am the figure of the temple yes this is true, however I am not and have never been a high priest that demands the compliance of his pupils, to be a dictator is not a position that I choose to hold at the temple. Some may feel that they have the right to impose their will on another, and those that do, their fates are in the hands of souls that are far more evolved than mine." Bion replied, he was being tested and he knew it.

"You say the earth-mother, as well as souls more evolved sees all, then why is this situation allowed to continue?"

"Are you saying that you will help?"

"Well, let's just say that I am here for now and that is enough." Petrus was trying not to commit but in his heart he knew that this was his destiny.

"Good enough." That was all Bion needed to hear. "The earth-mother says that this situation will play out no matter what she does to avoid the result." Bion continued. "All permeations lead down the same road so her only course of action is to allow this road to be travelled so that future generations can learn from the mistakes that have been made here."

"So you are saying that there is no hope for us?"

"Yes, that is what we are saying, but I know you already feel this."

That much was true. Petrus was feeling that if this situation continued, then it would end in pain for so many. The die was cast and from that moment on Petrus was to become a valuable and well-trusted man, true to his word with unwavering loyalty. In time, Bion was introduced to Petrus's brothers Ionas, Kallias and Miltiades, and between the four of them, they would prove to be a powerful tool against the priest, who was to challenge Bion.

The four brothers maintained a tight bond, holding a powerful link to each other that could not be penetrated. As a result, no man or woman could manipulate or use them against each other. They were as one.

One evening when Bion was at prayer, the earth-mother interrupted him:

"Bion, leave, leave now." It was the first time that she used verbal communication with him and he knew not to argue with her, he did not even look for provisions. He took a path that the earth-mother had been guarding, which he had been using to meet with Petrus. However, before he got to the opening, a hand grabbed him from behind and pulled him into the shadows. No more than a few seconds passed when armed guards entered the temple using the same route that Bion would have been travelling on. It was one of the brothers. Petrus and the other two were anxiously waiting in an empty house just outside of the city.

When Bion could relax, he turned to see Kallias. "Once again I owe you my life, my friend," he said, and then they made their way to the house to join the others.

Petrus was keeping a watchful eye on the whole situation via the link that he shared with his brothers, and on their arrival, they were greeted by smiles and hugs.

"How did you know? I was only warned late but you must have known much sooner."

"Yes, my friend. Kallias and Miltiades were in a tavern when they sensed the guard's energy and intentions. Kallias went for you. Miltiades linked up with us and the rest you know."

The brothers would often hang out at taverns and just blend in listening from afar. They were never questioned or suspected of any wrong doing, as they were well known for being mutes. It was a perfect situation for them.

By the time they left the house, Bion had tuned into the earth-mother he did have a little concern as to why he was warned so late about his pending situation. He knew that he couldn't go back to the temple, so he was in the hands of the brothers and the earth-mother, a situation that he found quite pleasing. The trek through the city outskirts was a long and interesting one for it was not a straightforward walk. The temple was being overrun with guards that were hired by the priest in his build-up to seize power from Bion. Priest's that were loyal to Bion were held captive in their chambers and there seemed to be guards on every street. By the time the men got to the gates, it was dark. This helped with their escape and gave Bion another chance to see the brothers' gifts in action. Using telepathy, they distracted the guards on the gate, giving them the opportunity to get through unnoticed. The distraction was made easier as the guards were hired from a lesser advanced race of people who were not familiar with the mental tools that the Lemurian people had developed over the years that they had followed the teachings of their benefactors.

When the group had cleared the city, and was clearly out of danger, Bion and Petrus took the opportunity to talk freely and discuss the way forward. Bion also took the opportunity to contact the earth-mother, feeling confident that he would get a direct answer, formed from the warning that he receive earlier that evening, he was not to be disappointed.

"I apologise for the haste and manner of the warning; however, I have prepared a place free from danger for you to shelter, and although I am aware that the brothers would want to stay close to the city, they will always be welcomed friends. You will also find that our bond will become stronger now that you are out of that city so full of stone and negativity, and in an environment that is more pleasing to me."

Bion was pleased with this message, yet he was a little confused as to why the guards got so close before he was warned. But when he considered what the earth-mother had told him he understood.

Earth-mother chose to communicate with Petrus using visions, which was a better way for him as he was such a powerful conduit. He could feel her love, which made the experience a more fulfilling one, not only for him, but for his brothers too. The advantage of this form of communication was that the thought, intention, emotion and intensity of the vision was untainted, so the true meaning of the message could be felt in the areas where it was directed, with no room for misinterpretation. This meant that the speed in which Petrus and his brothers improved their gifts and abilities was at a remarkable pace.

Before long they began to teach Bion how to further develop his mind and his knowledge of the forest. Petrus became a frequent visitor to the shelter and between them, they managed to document a wide variety of herbs and remedies with the assistance of the earth-mother and some unwilling volunteers. The worst affected of the volunteers was Ionas. Bion and Petrus would find ways of tricking him into taking what had been concocted, which at times was more than interesting to see the results. One of the more powerful remedies that was made helped Kallias to change his form. This was not expected and the earth-mother had to warn the men that they were stepping into realms that were not meant for this time. They were satisfied that they had done enough, and now they had a large collection of potions and remedies that would prove to be useful soon enough.

Bion was advised of a joining with Atlantis and the link between him and Ourania was established soon after that.

24
Tuesday
~~October~~
2020

It's
NOVEMBER

My opinion on our book: I'm 12 years old in year 8

FOR A WHILE I WAS INTERESTED IN THIS BOOK IT HAD A GOOD PLOT. BUT SOON I WASN'T VERY KEEN ON READING IT. I FOUND SOME NEW BOOKS THAT LOOK LIKE THEY WILL INTEREST ME BUT I FORGOT THE NAMES I'LL check later what they are. I probably won't. BUT IF I REALLY WANT THESE I'LL TRY AND GET THEM ON AMAZON.

Chapter Ten

The Foretelling

The party had reached the cavern safely. They were well out of danger and there was no reason why Petrus needed to keep Ianthe distracted any longer. Ourania and Bion were talking extensively about the forest and the energy fields. Despite the weight of their conversation, Ourania noticed how intently Ianthe was listening to Petrus, so much so, that she discussed the matter with Ianthe later that evening.

The dread that the women felt earlier in the month had long passed. Ourania told the men of their lives at Atlantis, a story that they found compelling.

"My brothers and I would love to visit there someday." The fact that Petrus would speak for his brothers seemed a little strange at first until the telepathic bond between them was explained fully. After a full telling of Atlantis had reached its conclusion, Petrus and Ianthe went in search for food, whilst the brothers kept themselves busy in and around the cavern.

"What are the brothers up to?" Ourania asked Bion looking slightly confused.

"Demeta wishes to address us after we have fed."

"They speak to her, too?"

"Not in the same way that we do," said Bion, "She talks to them in visions. They are more finely tuned into the planet than we are, which makes the vision speaking a much more direct and accurate way to communicate."

"Does this mean that they get the full emotion of the ʒage?"

"ʾhat's very perceptive of you, how did you know?"

"you know, I commune with Hypatia and have been for many years. When we communicate, I feel ʾl as talk to her. When she comes to me in my sleep time, I feel her more than hear her, and she tells me that it is a better way to communicate."

At that moment Petrus and Ianthe entered the cavern, placed the food on the earth table and everybody ate. After they had eaten, Petrus informed everybody that they had been asked to convene at the waterfall. When they arrived, they all sat on a grassed area and waited. Ourania could feel my presence and that of Hypatia. Ourania informed the others that they were being joined by two guests. In no time at all, our forms appeared in the circle of friends.

I was the first to come through: "I see we have some new strays to add to this union," I said humorously, to which Ourania gave an introduction.

"This is Petrus, Ionas, Kallias and Miltiades, who are Bion's friends, I have come to know them well this past month and already they have taught me much. Do you have any news that you wish to share with us?"

"I had talks with Hypatia before joining with you. We talked in depth about Kaius and the people that he is involved with. Hypatia has all but disconnected herself from Kaius, which has allowed us to consider the circle of people that he seems to be involved with, though it Hypatia can sense that she is being blocked by a strong, unnatural source."

"Will that not put you in danger?" Ourania asked.

"Well that's an interesting point, it seems that Hypatia had her own agenda all along. She knew that Kaius was trying to use her own power to shield his actions from her, or so he thought. She allowed him to think that he could master a power that was not his to master; however, for the elusion to hold true, she chose not to inform us of this fact. He has been scheming and plotting for quite some time. Hypatia has felt that the time is right for us to learn what is to come for our world, which is the reason why we have been brought to the circle."

"What of Maeja and Timo?" Ourania asked.

"Hypatia has sent them to the forest to talk with the animal kingdom. They need to commune with an old friend of theirs, a winged horse named—" before I could finish Ourania jumped in.

"Abraxas."

"You know him then?"

"I know of him; he was said to have been lost. He is as old as the crystal and it is said that he was blessed by the crystal."

Hypatia was waiting for this moment to pass, and when it did, she took incorporeal form and stood in the centre of the circle. "Honoured friends, the galactic command and I welcome you on this blessed day. I address you now as Hypatia keeper and guardian of the Akashic records for all life. I join now with Demeta to bring you this message for the world. The time for Lemuria is short. There will be no salvation for the people who have violated Demeta and she can no longer sustain equilibrium on the planet. She will unfold her skin to cleanse a blemish on her body, this will cause her lifeblood to rise and consume the lands of Lemuria and its people. All will not perish, some who have been true to the values of love will have the opportunity to travel, and they will be chosen to go to the four corners of the world. Some will go inwards. These are special souls that have proven themselves worthy to guard and respect the knowledge of these times. This knowledge will be kept until the earth is ready to live as it was intended to live. Some will reincarnate as dauphins. These will be special blessed children, who will help to protect hidden knowledge and assist in times to come with the healing of the planet. Some will travel to Atlantis to integrate with the people, and when that day comes, it will signify the ending of my time on this plane of existence. These people will be guided through visions as to their purpose and destination, those that are left will perish."

The whole gathering was silent but most had a tinge of sorrow in their hearts, Hypatia could feel this but continued nevertheless.

"From that day, Demeta will be the sole guardian of the planet we know as Tierra. And what of you, my blessed children. Ionas, Kallias, Miltiades Petrus, Ianthe and Timo will be the guardians of the inner kingdom. Bion, Ourania, Gaia and Maeja know their fate. You all continue to be an inspiration to both Demeta and I, you are living proof that the fate of this planet can be put back onto its correct path." Hypatia then passed the floor to Demeta.

"I thank Hypatia for her words. I, Demeta, watch with great sorrow at the way people treat each other. It brings me great pain to do what needs to be done, but it must be done to halt this flow of negativity. We in this circle know that life is a sacred gift, so my wish is for the fulfilment of the creator's plan for this blessed planet. It is the intention of the creator, for this planet to join with the procession of enlightened planets throughout the universe. I leave you and close this circle with that glorious thought, blessed be."

The circle was closed, leaving the seven of them to sit in quiet contemplation for a while before they made a blessing for this union.

Chapter Eleven

Maeja and Timo

With everything that had occurred over the years, Timo was feeling at a loss. She badly wanted to do something to help but felt that it was out of her hands. One day she spoke to me about her feelings, she knew I had a direct link to Hypatia, and Timo was hoping that Hypatia would give her some much-needed advice. What actually happened she was not prepared for?

"Priestess," she said, "I wish to do something more than what I am doing. I know that I play an important part in this, but I feel like I am not doing enough to help you."

I did not have to ask Hypatia as I knew that all that was said and done she was fully aware of; I could instantly feel Hypatia's energy coursing through me to give Timo her answer. I looked deep into Timo's eyes, as she listened to what Hypatia had to say through me:

"Finally, the child becomes a woman. I have been waiting for you, to ignite your true destiny, Timo. It was not by chance that you and your sister were brought to us as children. Timo, you are to go deep into the forest and seek out your father, he will guide you to Abraxas. You know of him in stories of legend that your mother would tell you and Ianthe at sleep times. From there you will have your answers you so badly seek. Maeja is to accompany you, for she and Abraxas are old friends. Abraxas came with the crystal to this planet, selected the first guardian to the matriarch and brought Maeja's mother to me. Their souls are and will be forever linked."

I repeated what Hypatia had told me to Timo, word for word. Maeja was out watching Kaius but was linked into the event so heard everything.

Timo was excited but kept her composure.

"May I tell Maeja?" I heard Maeja chuckled in my

mind.

"But of course you can." I didn't want to spoil her excitement, so I let Timo feel that this was a private moment that we shared, as there were times when Timo would forget the bond that I shared with Maeja.

***

Maeja was up early the following morning and left my chambers to wake Timo; as for Timo she was up unusually early, full of excitement at the prospect of being in her father's company again, she was running around her chamber getting herself ready. I had informed Maeja to come to me before they left to say their farewells.

On the way to the edge of the forest, Maeja could feel Kaius's presence. "Gaia, I can feel Kaius, he is close." Maeja had linked to me.

"Can you sense his intention?" I replied.

"He is preoccupied; he is waiting for someone."

"I will let Hypatia know, she will keep an eye on him," and with that, they continued with their journey, they travelled the whole day without rest, and the conversation was full and varied. That night they both slept extremely well. When they finally awoke, they were greeted by a group of animals that were just sitting and watching them. A young bear came forward and spoke to Maeja: "We have come to take you to Timo's father."

The animals were not sure if Timo had developed the link with them after spending so much time in the temple, but to their surprise it was Timo who replied:

"That will be just fine, thank you. Is he not at his home in the glade anymore?"

"No, he didn't like the energy that was coming from the city so he moved closer to us." Timo's mother had passed on twelve years previously; her father was now alone and chose to remain that way. The only reason why he stayed so close to the city was for his life partner's sake, to be close to her girls.

The bear turned to Maeja and they spoke in a tone that was for animals alone:

"One of our brethren has kindly offered himself to you as the journey ahead is a long one. You are well known to us, so it was an honour for him and he waits for you." They left the others and made their way to him. They walked for a short distance to an area where an old buck stood in waiting, Maeja was elegant in her approach and addressed this noble creature.

"Thank you for your generosity, I will not allow you to suffer."

Maeja knew the sweet spot on most creatures that would ensure a quick and relatively pain free death. She blessed the buck and asked for his soul to be removed before the kill. This would become a common ritual for Maeja, but this being the first, it was important to do this correctly. After the blessing was made she made the kill, which was swift and as promised, the deer did not suffer.

After Maeja had consumed what she needed to sustain her she washed her mouth of the blood in a nearby stream and re-joined the others who had already set off. For a lioness picking up their scent was easy, for an animal such as Maeja she could have done it with no sight at all. "Hallo, my friend." Timo acknowledged Maeja's arrival. "Did you have a good breakfast?"

"It was humbling to be honoured so," was all that Maeja could say. The whole episode had moved her deeply.

The remainder of the journey took three days. Maeja knew how to store the energy that the buck had given her and Timo ate as they walked for the forest was full of all manner of fruits, berries and nuts that she could feast on. Eventually, they reached a clearing, which seemed to be a circle. In the centre of the circle was a single oak tree that looked to be extremely old and wise. To the right of the oak tree stood a man, who Timo instantly recognised. "Father!" Timo exclaimed and then ran and jumped into her father's waiting arms.

"So, it is true my baby has come home. My friends have been here waiting for you both, and this magnificent specimen must be Maeja. I am honoured to meet you, as you are well known in the animal kingdom. My name is Silas."

"I too am honoured to meet the father of Timo." To find someone who could talk to Maeja who was not linked was a rare thing, although from the stories that Timo told Maeja on their journey, Maeja was not surprised.

"Father, we have come on a mission from the great crystal."

"I know, my child. I have been told. Hypatia talks to me regularly. I am to take you to Abraxas."

"I thought he was just stories of an animal long past but to see now that you actually know him…"

"Yes, Timo, I know him intimately. Do you remember the night before I brought you and your sister to the temple?"

"Yes, you and Mother were arguing."

"Yes, well it was Abraxas who instructed me to bring you to the temple, on the orders of the galactic command."

"What? It came directly from them?"

"There will be more time to talk on the way tomorrow, but now we must rest, for our journey will take us through mountains and valleys and will take four days if the goddess is with us."

Again, they slept well; being in the forest surrounded by nature was such a beautiful way to live. Timo had almost forgotten the serenity that nature brought to a soul if the soul was open to it.

When they woke, they found that Silas was already up. He had asked some rather tall horses to help with their journey, the horses understood the importance of their voyage, and they were more than happy to help. Timo wondered why she hadn't thought of that before, but was happy that her father had, as the journey ahead did in fact take four days and they rode all the way.

***

Abraxas was all that Timo had expected him to be, he was magnificent and made the horses that they arrived on look small and insignificant. He had a long flowing mane; his coat was the purest of white that it almost shone, he had a wingspan of at least twenty feet, with a horn in the middle of his head. The stories of his splendour paled in his presence, when he rose on his hind legs he was as tall as a house. Maeja and Abraxas greeted each other, he then turned to Timo and lowered his head in acknowledgement. With the formalities out of the way, they all sat to converse. Abraxas began by telling Timo and Maeja of his origins:

"My race was of a world that had no humans. Its name is Predrematea. We were visited by the being you know as the matriarch, she asked me if I would join her on this mission to educate this world, so that it may join with the procession of planets on the same evolutionary path. Our planet was seen as a pearl. Its inhabitants lived symbiotically and it was a perfect example of how things could be here on this planet. When it became painfully obvious that the plan for this world could not be realised, we had to go to extraordinary lengths to ensure that seeds could be planted for future generations to succeed where we had failed. Maeja, as I understand this, you know your destiny. It truly is a blessing and an honour.

"As for Timo and Silas, you will join Ianthe when the time comes. I will now share with you what has been decided for you all, you are all destined to travel to a place we refer to as Agartha. There you will learn so much and time will seem to stand still for you all who enter in this sacred place. You will build a great city with a population that will grow, knowing the true ways of an evolved race. Demeta will care for the people and they will want for nothing. There will be a select few, yourselves included, who will not age like normal people. This is ordained by Hypatia, Demeta and the galactic command. This serves to

90

ensure that the plan will be remembered and all will come to know you all as supreme beings.

"Ianthe, Petrus and his brothers Ionas, Kallias and Miltiades will be given the same gift. There is a soul that is destined to become your partner, Timo. You shall know him by his energy vibration, the same way that Ianthe has found hers. You will all be blessed and have children of your own, and when they are ready to take over from you all, you will be brought before the galactic command to receive your final blessing, which I am not at privilege to say."

Maeja and I did in fact know our destiny, which we had been aware of from a very early age. This was of great benefit to us, as it allowed us the power of foresight and wisdom beyond our years and it enabled us to develop at an unnatural pace.

Silas was overwhelmed on hearing the news and wept with joy. "Silas, my friend," Abraxas said, "why do you weep so? Do you not think that your place has been well earned?"

"I am no more than an old man who cares for his friends."

"No, not an old man, but a wise man who gave up his children because a power higher than his own asked him to. Did you question or refuse even when you knew it was breaking your beloved partner's heart, even when it was breaking your own? No, my friend, you have sacrificed so much for the good of your family and friends; you have shown loyalty and faith, and you have become a valued and trusted friend to me. Your knowledge and wisdom for the animal kingdom will be needed, but as for you being old, we have a special gift for you. Your heart is young so it only seems fitting for your age to match your heart. You, my friend, will remain here with me, and when the time comes, Timo, Ianthe, Bion, Petrus, Ionas, Kallias and Miltiades will make their way here to you."

The weeping turned into full-blown tears, Silas fell to his knees and thanked the heavens for allowing him the chance to see his beautiful daughters together again. He only wished that his love could have been there to see it. Maeja had known for some time what was to become of Timo and she was pleased that she no longer had to keep this from her. Maeja confessed to Timo that she knew of the plan and that she had known for years, to which Timo protested.

"You beast, some friend you are. I will never let you sleep by me again."

"Hmm, now I know you are not truthful, you will not keep warm without my fur when you sleep."

"That's true, maybe I will get my father to skin you, then I won't have your great weight crushing me."

"And who will protect you when you are alone?"

"I will find and train another lion or maybe I will get a tiger."

"Ah you would prefer a puppet over a companion."

"A puppet that wouldn't keep things from me."

"Oh, Timo, how far the apple has fallen from the tree. I never knew you could be so hurtful."

Abraxas and Silas looked at the pair of them, then each other, then back to them, at which point Timo and Maeja fell about laughing as this kind of banter they would have on a regular basis, then within seconds the whole group was beside themselves with laughter.

They spent another two weeks in the company of Abraxas where he would give them instruction of what was needed from them, and the need for the plans not to be revealed as it was explained:

"The people who will occupy Agartha will be shown the destination through visions. If this becomes common knowledge we will not be able to stem the flow of refugees, some of which will corrupt the beauty that is to be Agartha."

Two weeks later, Maeja and Timo headed back to Atlantis. Timo was so ecstatic that poor Maeja had to listen to a constant barrage of statements about the whole episode, yet she was extremely happy at the prospect of being with her father. Silently, she always missed his company, she never forgot his smile and the joy that being with animals brought him. Maeja's sensitivity picked up on this feeling and she questioned her about it.

"Do you regret your time at the temple?"

"Goddess no, Maeja, how could I ever regret the time that I have had at your side. Who would I have had to keep me warm on cold nights, when I have trouble sleeping?"

"Now you jest." Timo could tell by Maeja's tone that she was serious.

"Maeja, I would not turn back the time. I have learnt so much and made some very dear friends. I know that if I had stayed at my father's side, I would be loved and lived as my parents and their parents did, but I would not have realised my childhood dream to become a priestess. Yes, I did miss him and being with him these past days has re-sparked that desire in my heart, but I also know in my soul that this is where I belong."

"For now," Maeja said.

"Yes, for now, but it is still true to say I have lived a beautiful life and I will miss you and Gaia more than I have missed my father." Now there was a tear in her eyes. "Now look what you have done. I was so happy till now, so tell me where are you and Gaia going to be when I go off to Agartha?"

"I am afraid I am not at privilege to tell you now."

"Now – does that mean that you will tell me?"

"You're pushing and you know that does not work on me, so before you continue, best you watch your step." Timo was so consumed in the conversation that she was not mindful of the forest and the warning came far too late.

"Oh! Yuk! It's fresh and still warm." Maeja could do nothing but laugh, she was hysterical.

"That will teach you. If the powers that be wanted you to know, they would have told you. There is a stream over that rise."

Timo almost ran to the stream. She had forgotten the nature of things in the wild and had become used to the comfort of the temple. She sat on the edge of the stream and allowed the cooling water to run over her feet. Maeja caught up with her and sat beside her for a short time as she was still in a melancholy mood.

"Are you going to wash those or would you like me to assist you?"

"Yes please, that would be lovely."

"Yes please… I don't think so; it will never happen."

"Don't you love me?"

"Dearly, but my mouth isn't going anywhere near that."

"Point taken," Timo said.

Suddenly, a stallion appeared out of nowhere.

"Timo, Maeja; Abraxas has sent me. We must hurry. Gaia is of need of your assistance."

Without any hesitation, Maeja was up and running like never before. Timo got on the stallion, which took off with a speed that Timo had not witnessed before, she had heard of a breed of horse that had the speed of the wind but they were long lost to the lands of Atlantis. "What is your name?" Timo managed to ask.

"I am known by many as Trexus, and might I say you smell strange for a human."

Timo did not respond but she was concerned, as she could not see Maeja. "I am here, Timo, and making great haste." Maeja could feel Timo's concern and linked in to Timo. "There is no need for concern. I am nearing the city."

"Already?"

"I will explain later, but I feel Gaia's anguish. I must hurry." Maeja was a little disappointed with herself; she had allowed her link with me to weaken, an act that she would never let happen again.

Chapter Twelve

The More You Have

Maeja woke me up early the morning after Timo's meeting with Hypatia. She wanted to set off on the long journey to find Timo's father, Maeja had learned that he had left the nearby forest soon after Callidora, his life partner had passed on. Timo's parents were well known in the animal kingdom; in fact, they were akin to royalty.

Maeja left my chamber to join Timo, who was eagerly waiting in-between rushing around like prey trying to elude a hunter. I wanted to see Timo off so I informed Maeja to bring her when she was ready, I wanted them to try to relax and have some level of fun as we had all been totally focused on Kaius these past years, my duties did not allow for me the time to leave the temple and my companions were tied to me, so knowing that they had an opportunity to recharge gave me a sense of joy.

"Now the both of you find some time to have fun and stay linked at all times," I said. "Remember that these are troubling times."

Maeja and Timo said their goodbyes and were gone.

My chambers overlooked the city and from my balcony, I could see my friends departing. As I was watching them walking through the gardens I noticed Kaius. I also felt Maeja's concern as she contacted me, I in turn alerted Hypatia.

"Hypatia, Kaius is here?"

Hypatia watched Kaius constantly. His actions were becoming bolder and Hypatia knew that he would soon meet his fate. "I am watching, Gaia," Hypatia said. "It is as it seems. The time is upon us, so come to my chamber when the time is right."

I had some temple duties to administer before going to see Hypatia, and it was several hours later before I arrived at her chamber.

"I have been monitoring your energy this day, Hypatia, and it has been busy so what can you tell me?"

"Ourania has made contact with the final piece of her journey and the time is coming to join them. Both Demeta and I feel that you all need to know what is to come."

"What of Maeja and Timo?" I asked.

"Abraxas has been chosen to take care of the part that they are to play, he like me is well informed for what is to come. However, we must prepare ourselves for Kaius. We have allowed him to seal his own fate, which is now revealing itself. His lust for power and more knowledge is causing problems for the people that he is involved with. It seems that their patience is running out and they fear that his actions are causing their position to be illuminated. You, Gaia, must be the rock on which this temple is built. Kaius will attempt to follow the Lemurians' path, but we will not allow that to happen. This temple must stay unchanged. The Lemurian fate is serving a purpose and Atlantis will serve a similar fate but not yet. In the days to come, Kaius will note the absence of Maeja, and believe you to be vulnerable. As I continued to watch Kaius, a man arrived and they were in heated discussion. As for the man, he was talking to, I know little about him. He is shielded to me, which I find to be of great concern. The people who Kaius is involved with have attained some very powerful insights in governing that kind of power, which tells me that our time here is limited. From the energy that he was giving off, I could feel his displeasure in Kaius."

This was not new to me, and I totally understood what was being asked of me.

"Now the real tests will come," I said. "Please give me the strength to see this through."

I knew that my time as high priestess was soon to come to an end and the power and knowledge that I had accumulated would soon be put to the test.

"My sweet child," Hypatia said. "You command more

power than you realise." Even though I was well into my forties by now, Hypatia still referred to me as child, something that amused me greatly.

"Now the time has come to link in with Demeta and the others, for we have things to reveal to you all."

By the time I left the chamber and the link I felt like a weight had been lifted off my shoulders, but the elation of the meeting soon faded. I continued my duties throughout the passing weeks, and although I kept in contact with Maeja, my constant distraction in the form of Kaius saw the link getting weaker, a situation that I knew could be a problem. When I did try to strengthen the link, I found that somehow it was being blocked. *But why and by whom?* I consulted Hypatia about the matter but all that she said was, "If the need arises before their return, they will be notified. Also, this has happened for good reason; they both needed this time to rebuild and prepare for what they are being told."

It had only been two weeks since their departure and I was already missing their companionship. By now, I knew that Kaius was beginning to press his hand, and I was certain that he was going to attempt to take the crystal.

Macedon had also been quite busy; the lord was now contacting him directly as he had proven to be a loyal spy for the shroud. Nothing that Kaius did went unnoticed and the lord was most pleased with Macedon's reports but less pleased with the way that Kaius was handling himself. The lord had long guessed that the crystal had all but closed herself off to Kaius and thus, Kaius was getting desperate. He had overstepped the mark, even as high priest in the temple. The lord was shocked to hear the reports he was receiving from Macedon, but not surprised the elders had forewarned that this would happen, it was time to end this. It was time to find a new high priest and the lord felt that he had the perfect candidate.

***

It had been nearly four weeks since the departure of Timo and Maeja. Kaius was now pressing me hard for the joint control over the great crystal, and it was taking all my concentration to keep him at bay. Hypatia was beginning to become concerned for my safety and had asked Abraxas for the return of Maeja. To her joy, Abraxas reported that they had just finished what was needed to be done and they had left that morning.

That evening Macedon was given one last task to perform. He was given a black orchid. In Atlantis, there was only one person who grew this rare plant and it was the lord, who would only use them as a mark on a victim. It was his calling card, which was known only by the members of the shroud. Macedon was asked to place it on Kaius's table that night while he was asleep, a matter he felt should have been dealt with long ago.

Kaius woke up that morning in his usual bad mannered way, prepared himself for his daily duties and then sat down to eat. On the table in front of him was the sight that he had been dreading, and he panicked thinking about what he could possibly do to protect himself.

The crystal; yes the crystal and Gaia have power, he thought. *I have seen it. The priestess will help me, if she refuses I will take the crystal and leave the city.* He looked all over the temple to find me but to no avail. He thought that I must have been in the gardens, but again I was nowhere to be found. Finally, he went to my chamber, but found nothing. On leaving my chamber, he almost knocked me down as I had just left M's chamber and was on my way to the central chamber.

"Kaius, what is the meaning of this?" I said. "Is there something in my chamber that would see you in areas that priests have no grounds to be in?"

"I have no time for games or your condescending manner," Kaius said. "You will help me now or—" before he could finish I stopped him in his tracks.

"Or what? You will strike me down. Do you really think that you can force me to do anything against my will and the will of the crystal?"

"Enough, child. I am of need of the great crystal. I need her help."

"I will consult her," I said knowing full well that this was to be the time I had to be very careful from this point on.

"You play with me still, child," he said, and at this point, he pulled out a knife. I was already prepared for this and pushed him down, turned, and ran as fast as my legs would carry me to the central chamber. On my arrival, Hypatia closed and sealed the doors. Claritia and Chrysanta were inside the chamber and were shocked at my entrance and heightened state.

"High priestess, what brings you in here with such haste... and why are the doors sealed?"

All that I could say was, "Kaius." I stood directly under Hypatia and asked out aloud, "Hypatia, Maeja must be informed."

"I have told her already; she is on her way and Timo will not be long behind her."

Outside, Kaius was banging at the door and shouting but in vain. There was nobody who could help him get into the chamber except me. After a few moments passed, he left the hall and went to find Macedon, certain that he was behind the placing of the flower. He ran as far as his old legs could take him then walked at speed through the gardens where he met with Maeja. The crystal in the centre of her headpiece was glowing fiercely and she was in no mood to be polite. She roared a deafening roar that would have put even the bravest warrior on his seat.

There it is, Kaius thought, for he knew of the bond between his foes. He closed his eyes and waited for the blow that was to end his life.

"Maeja, no." There was no mistaking my voice. My link was back and it was stronger than ever. I could feel what was in Maeja's heart to do: "Come to me, Maeja. His fate is sealed and it will not be by our hands, so let the goddess deal with him."

Maeja left Kaius quivering in his clothes with his eyes still closed, she left as quickly and as quietly as she had come. By the time she had reached the central chamber, the doors had been released and the priestesses had gathered. Chrysanta was talking to me, she too was now very concerned about Kaius and was urging me to appoint a new high priest, I had given her instructions to leave the central chamber on Maeja's arrival.

Maeja ran into the chamber, a sight that none of the priestesses had seen, and on her arrival Chrysanta ushered the ladies out of the chamber. The crystal on her headrest was still glowing but not as brightly as it was in the garden. Maeja walked straight up to me and noticed that my wristband was glowing too.

"That's new, Gaia. Your crystal is glowing." I looked at my bracelet.

"Oh how strange," I said. "Come here." We walked to a polished metal plate and I held it up for Maeja to see her head.

"Oh my," we both turned to Hypatia, looked at each other and both said: "M's chamber." We went there directly. Hypatia had a tone and energy signature that would suggest that she was mildly amused at what Maeja and I had just discovered.

"And why are you amused so?" I asked calmly.

"Sorry," Hypatia said. "It's just that I have come to appreciate your childish humour. Please forgive me. I know that this was a testing moment for you both."

"So," I said, with a tone in my voice that gave a clear indication of my mood. "What is this that we are witnessing with the crystals?"

"These crystals are not of this world, there are twelve of them that were birthed from a special crystal again not from this world. When I came here, the matriarch instructed me that they were only to be used if the plan for this world could not be realised. You, Maeja, Timo and Ourania, each hold one. I am the mother of these crystals and the other eight are where they need to be. They have been implanting all that wear them with knowledge, strength, power and wisdom. They are your source, your seat of power, and they were also encoded so only someone who was worthy to wear them could do so. Such is the delicacy and meticulous planning that has gone into this moment right here right now, all is where it should be."

"Is this why I could span the distance that I just ran when Gaia was in trouble?" Maeja asked. She was a little shocked at how she had travelled so far and so quickly.

"Yes, my dear friend. These crystals are linked, but not in the same way that you share a link with Gaia. It is so much more than that. They were encoded to your genetic structure from the moment of your conception. Your link with Gaia is a by-product of their power. If Kaius knew this, he would have realised that all he needed to do was take one and with work and practice, he would have all the power he needed to rule this world and Gaia's life would have truly been under constant threat. When they sensed the danger that Gaia was in, the pair activated. This activation pulled you here; however, if you had the proper training, you would not have even needed to run."

"I must admit it did feel like I had all the power of the world in my paws," Maeja said.

"With training you will be able to move from one place to another with just a single thought."

I was now intrigued. "When will we be training for that then?"

"No, not here not now, that is for when we leave, to use that energy on this land in this time would bring too much unwanted attention to all of us, not only now but over the ages."

"Why was I not brought here using that mode of travel? Surely it would have been better if I was here much sooner." Hypatia could sense the frustration in Maeja's voice.

"You must remember that we have foreseen everything and at no time have we made any mistakes, to do so would mean this world would have perished long ago. At no time was there any fear that Gaia's life would have ended on this day. Your arrival was precisely what we wanted in the place that we wanted you to be in, to meet the person that you did. The love you have for Gaia is what keeps you both strong and the faith that you have put in me is what has kept the plan for this world strong and moving in the direction that was foreseen. The galactic command has given this earth the opportunity to try again in years to come. Demeta has permission to use Agartha as a sacred space for Timo and the others to store knowledge of what is to come. This knowledge may be used when the time is right for this world to be the pearl of this galaxy that it was designed to be."

Now my attention turned towards Kaius, as I felt a sudden change in his energy field. "Did you feel that, Hypatia?"

"Yes, I did, Gaia. The goddess has given him payment for his hard work." Kaius was dead.

Macedon found Kaius when walking through the gardens. He had suffered a heart attack; it was a slow death and as nobody was in the gardens, he died alone and in pain. Maeja's mood suddenly turned solemn as she felt that it was her fault and Hypatia knew she had to intercede or Maeja's guilt would come between us all.

"Maeja, don't do that to yourself. Look upon the wall and see what transpired."

The wall turned transparent like the clearest of crystals and with it, a picture started to form. To our surprise, there was Maeja standing in front of Kaius, roaring that menacing roar. If not for the seriousness of the mood in the chamber, the pair of us would have been laughing at the look on Kaius's face and the fact that he was leaking from his undercarriage.

Maeja left, and then Kaius opened his eyes and sat for a few minutes. He got up to leave, but was greeted by the same man that Gaia had seen in the gardens many weeks before.

"Maeja, that's the man I saw him with when you left."

The vision continued. The man touched Kaius's shoulder and said: "Your time is done," and walked away. Within seconds, Kaius was in early stages of arrest.

Together Maeja and I said, "That man is a wicked man."

"I fear that we have not seen the last of him," I said.

"I fear that you are correct," Hypatia replied. "And as I know little about him, I can only suggest that he has an unnatural and negative aura around him, as his energy is muffled. I sense great darkness in him. We must strengthen our link from now on. I will consult with the galactic command but from now on, we must stay vigilant. Ah, Timo has arrived, you have much to discuss with her, so go to her now, for she is in distress."

Trexus ran as fast as he had ever run, it was true to say that although he was a horse, his race of horses was mythical in the sense that his race was known to be able to run at such a pace, that time would seem to stand still, the remainder of his race had long left the surface under the guidance and advice of Abraxas. Trexus himself knew that Maeja was special, but for a lioness to outrun a horse, was unheard of in the animal kingdom, but for a horse such as he. *How I will never live this down*, he thought to himself.

Maeja and I were in the gardens waiting for Timo. I had never thought of Timo as anything more than my personal priestess. So, to see her on a horse galloping through the garden was a splendid sight to see. Trexus came to a halt and Timo dismounted, stroked his head and thanked him. "Thank you, my friend. I may have need of your assistance again someday. Can I rely on you to come if I call?"

"It will be my honour," Trexus said. "But only if my embarrassment stays between us. To have Maeja beat me to the temple is just too much."

Timo laughed. "Oh, my friend. Maeja is special. We all know that."

At this point Maeja stepped in: "Trexus, fear not. I had

assistance. It was not my legs alone that brought me here but have no fear, this secret will not leave us."

Trexus was relieved: "Thank you, Maeja. I am in your debt."

We informed Timo of what had just transpired, whilst walking over to where Kaius's body lay. Macedon was still with him, along with the head priestess and three priests, who were assigned to administer the dead. The priests confirmed that his heart gave up on him and wrapped his body to prepare it for the passing-on ceremony. On the way, back to the temple, I informed Timo that all their energy must go into the preparation for the days to come. With the information that she had received from Abraxas, Timo was under no illusion that what was to come was of great importance, and as such, she felt that she had to work hard to become all that she could be.

Chapter Thirteen

The Elders

Kallicticus was not a native of Atlantis, but he had asserted himself into a position that gave him access to the temple. On arrival to the Atlantean shores he studied the civilisation and soon found that he could work his way into the temple through means of supplying the temple with works from fashioned gold. He manipulated what was the master craftsman for the temple which is to say that he caused his early death, then after a short period he was introduced to the temple as a master of gold, highly skilled, this was all designed and carefully planned to a point that enabled him to be close enough to the temple without being seen. His work was often commissioned but he made a point of never meeting the people of the temple, he would always use his students. If his presence was requested by the temple, the message would simply be that he was finishing off a piece of work or he was sourcing gems and gold for his work.

Kallicticus arrived at the cavern at dusk and followed the path to the meeting point, took one of the torches from the wall and proceeded to walk past the pedestal to an opening at the back of the cavern. From there, the path ran down to a deeper cavern. The air was stale and warm with no light, Kallicticus placed his torch on the wall and knelt in front of six men who were sitting on stools in darkness. These men never left the cavern and seemed to live on water alone; their skin was translucent and thin, because they never came out of the cave in daylight, their eyes were glazed in appearance. These men were masters of the dark arts and had long plotted to gain control over the crystal. Kallicticus was their only student and although he had surpassed their skill level, he still feared and respected them.

"Is it done?"

"Yes, master," Kallicticus said. "He breathes no more."

"Were you seen?"

"No, master."

"We are pleased; will he be ready to take his place?"

"Yes, all has been prepared as instructed. He is eager to serve."

"That will be all," and with that Kallicticus left.

These men were ex-priests of the temple. Their duties were to keep the gardens and plants, to gather and prepare the food, to collect the guardian animals for the birthing ceremony, and to keep records of the temple's many occupants and for the city.

Aaron was the most adventurous and the first to start to question the power of the crystals. His questions soon reached the high priest of the time, who made the decision to banish him from the temple. Aaron had friends and they too were sought out and banished. It was felt that they left the area and went to distant lands, on their travels they came across a civilization that pre-dated their own. They were extremely happy to learn that males held the power in these lands, and these people seemed to be connected to a power source much like Atlantis, they had found Lemuria.

The priests of Lemuria learned that these men were in fact priests from a distant land and indoctrinated them into the order, where they studied hard. In a short time, they surpassed their teachers and wanted more power than these priests could show them. Discontented and knowing that there was more power to be had, they left Lemuria in search of a greater source of power. Eventually, they came to an island that practised the dark arts, in which they became totally immersed in the practice of dark magic. Many of them perished by the hands of their companions, and only the strong were to survive. By now they were practising on such a level, it seemed that nothing could surpass them. With all that they had acquired they knew that there was one thing that would stand in the way of what they were planning. Time would not be an ally to them so they sought out a Shaman, he was believed to have the power to stop the ageing process. However, it was also known that it would come at a price, that price being a person's soul. His name was Isingoma. When all the deals were struck, they made a pact to return to Atlantis and learn what they could about the great crystal.

On their return journey, they came across a young orphan boy. They could see in him a darkness and ability that they knew they could exploit. The boy's name was Kallicticus, who at six years old had the ability to do sleight of hand magic. They would teach him simple things, yet nothing that would endanger him; as for the boy he was hungry for knowledge and power, the bond that grew between the men and the boy formed quickly and naturally. It did not take long before they introduced him to darker magic. By the time they reached Atlantean shores, he had developed into quite a powerful individual.

The remaining men knew that the people of these lands could communicate with most things, as a result they decided to spend their days resting and practise their art during the night, this took its toll on their appearance. Bright light had become a problem to them, and because of the lack of natural light on their skin, they had a look of the dead.

It had been many years since they had left Atlantis and much had changed. There had been a succession of high priests and priestesses, up to the point of Hermione, the high priest posed an interesting prospect to them. He seemed a little outspoken towards the duties of the priests at the temple, so the plan was made to introduce Kallicticus to the temple to keep an eye on him and learn if there were any other disillusioned individuals at the temple.

When they first arrived in Atlantis, they lived in the forest, but found that it did not serve their purpose. There was too much light to begin with and the chatter of the animals was distracting.

So, using their magic, they found a place that would allow them to practise some terraforming, a task that they had acquired by way of a powerful sorcerer. They formed a path and manipulated the land to terraform a cave, which they knew would serve them better as they intended to grow their numbers.

After spending a few months watching Kaius, it was decided that he would be approached to see if he was committed to his belief. One morning he found a note on his table, which said: 'If you believe in what you want, we may be able to help. Come to the base of the mountain on the far side of the glade at high dark.'

Kaius was the first to be recruited. The elders changed their appearance and made themselves look one hundred and forty years younger. They met after dark, as this was when they were at their strongest. After Kaius was recruited, the remainder of the members came quickly; everything was moving along splendidly, in the forming of this rather select few, some carefully placed whispers pertaining to a leadership of the group was introduced, and it became known to the members that there was a leadership that went by the simple name of the elders, as for who they were that was always a closely guarded secret. When the group would meet, the elders would blend in and not reveal themselves. They would mingle in with the members and read them to see if they were still worthy. If they were found to be weak, then they would fall ill and die, and that task would be left for the young apprentice Kallicticus, and unlike the elders his presence was known but his face was always shielded.

It soon became apparent that they needed to do more work to protect the cave. They used some powerful magic to put a cloak on the cave, and if anybody strayed onto the site, all they would see was a rock face. As for the crystal, she would sense nothing. To maintain this cloak of invisibility, they needed to make a separate cave so they could continue their studies and expand on what they knew. Again, this was cloaked, so that only Kallicticus knew of its existence.

The elders knew that the time would present itself when Kaius would need to be silenced. The elders also knew that Kallicticus would be in full agreement for he was a loyal subject. Not once did Kallicticus have reason to question their orders or judgements.

As time went by the elders relied on Kallicticus to take care of the locals, whilst they worked on the crystal. It was an arrangement that suited both parties. Kallicticus would come to them every night and at times help them with their work; keep them apprised of any problem members, or if he had to silence any of them, and they would inform him if there was anything that they needed from him or the members. All was going well until a meeting was called and the whole situation was deemed unacceptable. First to arrive on that day was Kallicticus and went directly to the elders.

"That fool has summoned the members without our knowledge or approval. He assumes to use the shroud for his own. To call for a meeting in full daylight... I will cut him down in front of the members. He assumes too much."

"Leave him be for now," was all that was said, all the elders agreed. One of the elders shifted his appearance and went up top. To his horror, Kaius was adamant about what he wanted to see happen to the new priestess. Not a lot was known of this priestess, except that her training was not standard and that the great crystal was constantly blocking their vision of her.

Aaron was the priest who went to see why this meeting was called, and more so, as it was called in full daylight. He had heard enough and turned to Kallicticus, who knew exactly what to do. Aaron cloaked himself and went back to join the other elders, who all instinctively knew that they had to check the cavern for any energy that could have penetrated the cloak on the cave. When they were happy, they went back to work on trying to weaken the crystal. They were less than happy about what had transpired, but they also knew that this would prove to be a good distraction for the crystal, which they were sure would be looking at Kaius.

Kallicticus had kept his identity a secret under advisement of the elders to the membership, which was simply called the shroud. He was known as the lord, and when the shroud was in session, he would wear a mask. This gave him the ability to keep a check on the members for their loyalty and discretion, which could mean their very lives. He had gained a reputation for being able to end a person's life without using force and he was not afraid to use this power. In the early days when initiates were first gathered, many would suddenly die.

Many years had now passed since that incident and Kaius was allowed to live as it served a purpose; however, his access to the shroud was very limited in the years that followed. From the many meetings that were called, he only attended two of them. The members were told that their dealing with him must be purely business of a mundane nature, but not shroud business, and from that moment on Kaius's standing in the shroud was weakened.

Soon after that day, Kallicticus was made aware that one of the members was looking for a meeting with the lord. The method for initiating a meeting with the lord took a couple of days. As nobody in the shroud knew what he looked like, the message would travel from place to place until it got to the spot under a rock on the edge of the city, by which time Kallicticus already knew of its existence and did not even need to go to the spot. As soon as the note was placed under the rock it would disintegrate but the writing would manifest in Kallicticus's hands when he was ready to receive it. It was Macedon and he was pleading for his life, swearing loyalty to the shroud and claiming his innocence for the incident with Kaius. Kallicticus knew in an instant that this would prove to be very useful and the following day he left a note instructing one of the members to visit with Macedon and let him know that his services would be needed.

The elders knew that one day Kaius would need to be

silenced, but they needed another to take his place. They could not afford the chance of a high priest that they could not control. In the membership, they had four priests from the temple, and one of them was a perfect candidate for the position. Kallicticus agreed that this man had indeed stood out. He was ten years younger than Kaius and had all the training that Kaius had, and his wisdom and advice was thought to be of greater value. Kallicticus watched him with great interest and the elders put a shield around him as all agreed that when the time was right, he would be the one to take over from Kaius.

Many years had passed now and Kallicticus was getting weary of Kaius's childish ways. It was time to talk to him, and he went directly to Kaius knowing that from that moment on, he would not have the time to inform anybody of his identity. He sent word for Kaius to meet with him in the gardens in the early morning so that all would be sleeping. In the meeting that followed, Kaius was instructed to relinquish his role as high priest and Kallicticus knew that Kaius's pride would not allow him to do this, so they argued for a short while.

"Who are you to tell me what I should do with my life," Kaius said. "Why are you wasting my time?"

"I am a messenger for the lord," Kallicticus said.

Maeja and Timo had sensed his energy earlier and alerted me, so I called Hypatia, who was already aware of his presence.

Kallicticus did what was needed to be done. He would leave an orchid for Kaius soon.

Chapter Fourteen

The Path Before Us

The event that unfolded in the central chamber left Maeja feeling uneasy. She had questions for Hypatia and I could feel my friend's concern. "Go to her, Maeja, I will have words with Timo, for she too needs questions answered."

Maeja walked at a gentle pace to M's chamber, her mind was full of questions, and she wanted to fully get her emotions in check before being with Hypatia alone. Inside the chamber Maeja sat for a while in quiet contemplation; after what seemed like an eternity, Maeja got up and turned to leave, expecting to pass through the wall as we always did, she found that her path was blocked and she hit her head. Hypatia broke out in a full-hearted laugh. Maeja was not amused, she roared to show her annoyance which made Hypatia laugh even harder, when she calmed down Hypatia asked, "Why are you so vexed, Maeja?" Maeja's reply was abrupt and rude.

"You knew I wished to leave."

"Check your emotions, Maeja, we are friends are we not?"

"Apologies, Hypatia, but you jest with me when you know I am in no mood to jest."

"There is always room to jest, Maeja, especially when it is needed to help with a painful situation."

There was still humour in Hypatia's voice but with a serious undertone.

"Now, Maeja; you come to my chambers to seek a private audience, yet try to leave without a single thought or word, I thought you knew me better than that."

"You know I am troubled yet you say nothing. You know what is in my mind, yet you wait for me to speak."

"Did you not come to me? Yes, I could make it easy for you but this is not the way of it. You wish for understanding do you not? You must first understand what you are looking to understand. To do that you must put the words forward; this will help you to achieve understanding of that which you wish to understand."

"Hypatia, that was truly the most confusing thing I have heard you say in our private chats." Now they both were laughing, Hypatia had designed it that way, to promote the exact response she just received but she knew that it would make sense to Maeja in the end.

"There, that's much better; now we can talk, so tell me, Maeja, and take your time for there is much to cover, what troubles you?"

"Was it known before we left for the forest, that this was going to happen?"

"Yes it was."

"Did Gaia know?"

"No, she did not."

"Then why was this allowed to happen? And why was my link so weak, that it had to take Abraxas to warn us?"

"There are events that have already been written in our energy fields that are designed to strengthen us, and to teach us to be mindful of deception. It was necessary for the three of you to feel this anguish to help prepare you for what is to come."

"What about the link?" Maeja asked.

"We had to weaken the link," Hypatia said. "It was our intervention. Timo is an important part of the road forward, and for that reason, we needed to ensure that there were no distractions. We had to allow you to go with her to force Kaius's hand so he could reveal the shadow behind his movements; unfortunately, it seems that the man we saw was not at the top of the tree. I promise you, Maeja, at no time did the galactic command stop protecting Gaia. She was given the strength to cope with whatever came at her, much like you were given the speed, strength and stamina to get here so fast."

"So, does that mean that there is still a threat to you?"

"Yes, my friend, but we are working on remedying that

situation."

"Are the crystals that we wear able to do more than just give us what you have described?"

"Yes, they can, there is much power in these crystals, and as I have said before, they have the power to cause a lot of harm. However, Maeja, until you are in a safer place, I will not say another word on this subject. I have an adviser, a guardian you might say, who lives on Nibiru with the galactic command, together we have the knowledge to manipulate time to see all permeations that could exist at a single moment in time."

"Are they close?" Maeja asked she was clearly intrigued about this mysterious Nibiru.

"Nibiru sits in another dimension. This planet sits in a three-dimensional plane, Nibiru sits on the fifth dimension, a dimension that this world is destined for."

"I have heard of this place."

"But to answer your question, yes, they are close."

"Thank you, Hypatia. I have been educated and my mind is at rest."

Maeja turned to leave but she stopped at the wall not certain if her passage was clear.

"Yes Maeja you are free to leave." Hypatia confirmed, still with humour in her voice. With that, Maeja made her way back to my chambers.

**

"Did you get the answers you required?" Maeja had entered my chambers. The head priestess had insisted that we stayed in my chamber to get some rest. Two priestesses stood watch at the door, and had food brought to the chamber, I had finished with Timo but she stayed more out of guilt than duty.

"Yes," Maeja replied. "I did and it was most insightful."

"Yes we know, we particularly liked the part where you walked into the wall."

Timo and I laughed so much that it hurt our insides, when we had composed ourselves Maeja spoke.

"That was supposed to be a private meeting, how was it that you were able to see all?"

"Our crystals, Maeja, our crystals; even Timo saw and heard everything."

From that moment on between the three of us, we were to receive a series of visions, that was to guide us for what was before us, and how we were to prepare. The person who seemed to have the most to do was Timo, for it was revealed that along with her sister, father, Petrus, and his brothers, they were to be matriarchs of Agartha.

Maeja and I were to assist Timo in learning about energy and crystal healing. During her time as caretaker of Hypatia, she had witnessed many wonders but it was not her place to question what she had seen, or try to understand it. Ianthe was getting a similar set of instructions from Petrus. Petrus was instructing her in the art of looking into people's energy fields to detect their intentions, an act that she grasped quite quickly. However, she did not reveal it to Petrus, as she could see what his energy was portraying, which she discussed with Ourania.

Ourania had long seen the bond between them growing, so she was not surprised when Ianthe put the question to her.

"You are not a priestess anymore," was Ourania's reply. "You are free to follow the path that the goddess has set out for you." Ianthe blushed but thanked her.

Ourania helped Bion and studied hard so she could relay the information back to me. Bion was heavily involved with the brothers whenever they would come to the cavern, grasping what the brothers had learnt about what was going on in Lemuria. It seemed that people were getting restless and Bion's influence and presence at the temple was sorely missed. A faction of priests who had stayed loyal to Bion, helped people who wished to leave the city. They would have secret gatherings in people's homes and sometimes the discussions would become heated. Bion was also told that some people were taken from their homes, brought to the temple, and tortured for information. At first, this would start in the dead of night, but lately they had begun to take people from their homes during the day.

Ourania took Bion to one side; "You know how this will end don't you."

"I fear I do," Bion said. "Is there truly nothing we can do about this?"

"I am afraid it is out of our hands, my friend. We all know what we must do for the future of humanity. I know they are your people and some are your friends, but Hypatia was quite clear: we cannot help a soul. Hypatia and Demeta will guide the worthy to a safe haven." Bion had tears in his eyes. "Oh, my friend, we have to concentrate on the task at hand and stay on the right path."

"Stay on the right path," Bion repeated, with that they went to the pool to re-energize and re-focus.

That night they all received visions in their sleep, which portrayed vivid images of what they were to do. Ourania was first to wake, and on doing so she asked Liya to join her.

"Liya, my friend, go to Leonidas. He will know what to do."

Everybody who was linked to this group was now in a position where they knew that their time in the lands of Lemuria was limited. The three brothers took one last trip to the city as a request from Bion to assess that all was indeed as it seemed and to return as quickly as possible for a journey to the coast. When they returned from the city, all were now ready for the trek to the coast. On leaving their haven, they all turned and thanked Demeta for her hospitality and waited for her response. At that point, the cave was gone and so too was the pool and waterfall. The energy had shifted, returning everything to its original state; even the ley line, the power source, was withdrawn back to its resting place. The time had come to set off on their journey toward their final destination.

Chapter Fifteen

Silas

The trip to the coast took five days, they walked at a more gentle pace and took the time to talk extensively about what would be waiting for them in Atlantis. When they arrived at the coast they waited a further one day for Leonidas to arrive with the help of Liya. They used this time to gather food for the voyage back to Atlantis, and when Leonidas arrived mid-morning, he looked happy to see Ourania.

"Have you been waiting long?" Leonidas asked.

"No, we arrived yesterday morning, which gave us time to gather food for their journey."

"Their journey, priestess?"

Ourania took him to one side, "I will not be coming, my friend. My work here is not finished."

"I have heard stories of the people here, and how they are being treated in this mad man's attempt to find you and your companions. I fear for your safety, priestess."

"I follow the will of the goddess, my friend. I will see you again in the hereafter."

Leonidas didn't want to hear this, but he knew of the nobility of her life as a priestess. It soon became apparent to Ianthe that Ourania would not be joining them. Bion had known for a short while but there was something in the way she was acting towards everybody, and in the unions of souls, the messages were at times quite cryptic.

Ianthe had no shame in what she was about to do and it was the first-time Ianthe used Ourania's name, the words just came out with no filter.

"Ourania, what are you doing you cannot stay, what are you thinking? Bion, tell her please. Tell her she must come with us. Please. No, priestess." Ianthe was now inconsolable. "Priestess, please, please... have I not served you well? Am I being punished? Surely, the great crystal can't want this for you. Please, priestess, there must be a mistake?"

Ourania looked at Bion, who was now crying but took a hold of Ianthe, and then Ourania turned away. "No! Somebody stop her! She is my life and my soul. She cannot stay please no, no, no."

Everybody felt her pain. Bion was holding on as tight as he could. Eventually, Petrus and Miltiades had to help him as her struggle was getting too much for an old man.

On the ship, the crew stopped work at Ianthe's plea, as each one of them felt the pain that she was feeling in their hearts, something that neither one of them would ever forget. Liya flew off the mast that she was perched on after Ourania had turned a bend and went over a dune, to fly to her. As Ourania walked away, she felt every shriek of pain that Ianthe cried out. She was desperate to turn back just to hold on to Ianthe and give her strength to let Ourania go. *"Oh please, goddess. Give me the strength to carry on."* Ourania said to herself, clearly weakened. When she went over the dune, she put her hand over her mouth so they would not hear her cries.

Ourania began to feel Hypatia's energy. "Please not now, Hypatia." Until now, she had never refused Hypatia, but this was something that she wanted to face alone; nevertheless, Hypatia stayed close. If Ourania was to continue on this path, she wanted to use this pain to give her the courage to see it through to the end.

"Liya," Ourania said. "Stay close to Ianthe. She will need you. You will take her to Abraxas. Hypatia will show you the way, it is my time. As for you, Liya, you will serve a greater purpose. Now, stay close to Ianthe, and in time if she wills it, you will become her companion."

***

Silas and Abraxas spent the first few days talking about what was going to be lost. Abraxas was a dear friend to

Silas's family due to the work that they did for the animals. It went back generations and Abraxas knew the whole lineage of Silas's family, for it was Abraxas who taught the first line of his lineage the art of animal healing.

"We who are connected to the galactic command extend our gratitude, not only to you, but also your kin past, present and future. Because of the personal sacrifice that you made, what was lost shall be regained. This is a promise, but now we have to prepare for the gathering."

Silas did not know of what Abraxas was speaking, but knew to trust him, as he did when he was asked by Abraxas to bring his daughters to the temple.

"Follow me, Silas, this is the reason why I have been up here all these years."

They walked up a mountain pass, which opened into a hidden entrance to a tunnel. In the tunnel they must have walked for almost a day; as they walked they seemed to go deeper into the earth, they reached a spot where a resting place had been carefully prepared. There was food and bedding there, Silas ate his fill and had no difficulty in sleeping. When he awoke, he was totally revitalised and ready to continue his journey. Abraxas was pleased with Silas's recovery and pushed on; this would continue for four days until they came to a huge expanse, it was as big if not bigger than Atlantis – there was warmth, earth, stone, plants and animals. The animals had long sensed the arrival of Abraxas and all came to greet him, they bowed and gathered around Abraxas and Silas, then raised up and stamped their front legs. The noise was immense but beautiful at the same time.

"They know of you, my friend, and they are pleased that you are here with them," Abraxas said. Abraxas then looked at two bears and nodded his large and noble head, they walked up to Silas, stood up on their hind legs and held him firm. Silas had a little fear in his heart but that was soon put to rest.

"Silas, do not fear, not a single animal here wishes you harm, for you are well known and these animals insisted that you be part of the plan. What will happen now is I will implant the knowledge of all the animals that are here in this place and the ones that will join us over a period of time. The bears are here to support you and stop you from falling, trust that all is what it should be." Silas relaxed and prepared himself for he didn't know what or how it would happen. Abraxas walked to Silas, bowed his head and gently touched his horn on Silas's forehead between his eyebrows and as he did Silas felt weakened as if to faint, the images that flooded into his brain were overwhelming but gentle. He did indeed faint and when he came to he was lying on the ground; waiting patiently next to him lay a single white tiger by the name of Nikador and she was a beauty to be sure, she lay next to Silas to keep him warm.

"Steady, Silas, that was a lot for you to take in. Abraxas is close, and I will take you to him, I am to be your guardian my name is—" Before she could finish Silas interrupted her,

"Your name is Nikador and you will take me to Abraxas when I have regained my strength; thank you, Nikador." Silas showed an eagerness to go, so without delay Nikador took him to Abraxas.

"Hallo my friend, how are you feeling?" Abraxas was clearly pleased to see Silas.

"Very well and feeling very rejuvenated."

They spent a further eight months in the cave that was known as Agartha, until Abraxas could feel the pending arrival of the Atlanteans at the gathering area.

"Silas we have to leave this place and get things ready for the gathering and I have a treat for you." He dropped down in an almost kneeling position, "Get on, we are not leaving the same way that we came."

Now Silas was excited to have the honour of riding such a noble animal. Abraxas stretched out his huge wings and took to flight, which made Silas fear for his life and made Abraxas laugh. "I have wanted to do this since you arrived. Hold on tight, my friend. I would hate to have to explain to Timo that I lost you."

Silas laughed and gave out a cry of joy, and thinking, *if only his beloved could see him now*. They rose higher and higher.

"Are we not going the same way that we came?" Silas asked, and then his curiosity turned to fear.

They were heading toward the top of the cave, then suddenly, the ceiling vanished to expose blue sky. When they were clear of the cave, Silas looked back to see what looked like the crater of an old volcano. Abraxas stopped flapping his wings, stretched them out and allowed the wind to take them. He was so graceful yet powerful, and as they glided down to the bottom of the mountain Silas's joy could be heard throughout the vicinity, Silas jumped off Abraxas, adrenaline causing his legs to give way from under him.

Abraxas laughed: "Take your time, my friend, lest you fall and harm yourself."

Now Silas sat and allowed the moment to truly take a hold, and in that moment, he felt truly blessed.

Chapter Sixteen

Timo

Hypatia, Maeja and I started the training for Timo. She did possess a fair amount of knowledge, but what she truly needed was a full account of the power of the crystals, alongside with their true value and importance. What followed was an intense crash course that totally immersed the four of us. Timo was an excellent student, she studied hard and the questions that she would ask helped not only her but me also. Occasionally, the head priestess would lend a hand, especially when Maeja and I had temple duties to conduct.

One such duty was the appointment of a new high priest, with all that had been going on in the times that Kaius was still serving the temple, there was one man that I felt could make a good replacement if Kaius's attitude got out of hand. This priest seemed to have the ear of the order, and it seemed that most if not all would go to him before they would go to Kaius. I watched this situation with great interest in times when my attention was not being pulled in the direction of Kaius. I was approached by the head priestess about the matter as it seemed that an appointment needed to take place and soon. With all that I had seen there was something in the back of my mind that niggled me, although this man stood out amongst the remaining possibilities, I felt that there was something not quite true with this man, my intuition was telling me not to rush into a decision. Hypatia was aware of the request made by the Chrysanta and was also aware that I would not commit to giving her an answer; more importantly, she knew that there was a candidate on route that was planned for. Eventually Hypatia questioned me on this matter at great lengths, but until I could give her a justifiable reason why I was reluctant to allow the position to stand, Hypatia was going to allow it to continue; it was a delicate game that she was playing, a game that I was blinded to. I asked for the appointment to be postponed and to my surprise, Hypatia agreed without too much fuss. However, she informed me that I had three weeks in which a decision needed to be reached, and if I failed to produce a clear reason why, then Hypatia would allow the posting to stand.

Maeja could also feel that the man was not right for the post but she was confused as to why Hypatia was so reluctant to listen to me. It was the first time that Maeja had seen us at opposing sides of a decision, something that I was most uncomfortable with.

I needed some quiet time to meditate and search my feelings on the subject and went to the gardens to relax. When I entered a deep meditation, the first thing that came to me was Bion. I saw him in the forest with animals surrounding him and he was talking to them. I was aware that he was telepathic, but I was not aware that he could communicate with the animals. Then I saw him in the temple with priests and priestesses around him, closely followed by the soon-to-be new high priest, who was talking to the wicked man in the garden.

That was it! He was linked to the people who had killed Kaius. Now that I had the information I needed, I went directly to see Hypatia.

"Hypatia, I now know why I had questions about the would-be new high priest, he is linked to our problem."

"Thank you," she said. "I was beginning to worry that you would not get there."

"You mean to say that you knew?"

"Yes, I did. But I had to let you find out for yourself."

"Now you have lost me?"

I needed a better explanation than that as I could have made a terrible error, and it seemed that Hypatia was going to allow this to happen.

"Had you have followed my instruction, then you would not be doing your job as high priestess, you would have become a puppet and would not be using the very gift that makes you who you are. Your intuition is a gift, but to use it without knowing the reason why is foolish. It is important to follow it but this can lead to a road of destruction without the use of knowledge, but knowledge alone is not enough. You must be a wise leader, knowledge with wisdom can also be a potent recipe for making bad decisions but to have knowledge and wisdom, used with reason and feelings, then applied logically, leads the seeker to answers fully informed, and in a place to do what is correct for all concerned. Even though I knew he was not the correct candidate for the post, I had to make sure you knew but also know the reason why. Now I ask you if we do not allow the posting to continue what do you think will happen?"

"I am not at all sure, I didn't stop to think."

"Exactly, which is why I gave you the opportunity to seek the answer to the question that you have been asking. This priest is indeed part of the people who wish us harm and he will, if allowed to do so, work his way into our inner sanctum. If we close the door on him with no good reason, it will tell the people that wish for him to take over Kaius's position, that we know of them and that will produce a much more volatile position for all of us. Yes, we do have the capability to ward off any attack that is directed our way, but how will that affect the stability of Atlantis? How many would perish in the wake of a rebellion?"

"Would it come to that?" I asked.

"Knowledge, wisdom, reason and feelings, this an important lesson for you to learn, Gaia; yes it could come to that and if it did the population of Atlantis would suffer greatly."

The ceremony was postponed and when the question was asked the response was that I was in consultation with the great crystal. What now followed was for a possession of candidates to put their points forward for their personal advancement to become the next high priest. I listened closely to all the arguments put forward by the candidates, to which I explained that due to the sudden death of Kaius, I felt his successor was not properly prepared so all candidates for the high priest had to pass all tests put before him, tests that Hypatia was to put forward in the correct manner at the correct time, as it has always been in times past. However, this was a ruse as I felt that the true reason was yet to present itself, and that would happen soon, and yet again Hypatia left me in the dark pertaining to Bion, due to the fact that I did not seek clarification on my vision, I had my answer about the candidate so did not pursue the link concerning Bion.

***

The training of Timo was moving onto higher levels, and now she was being guided through visions to specific areas where powerful crystals could be located. Timo did not question the source of the visions although there were times when she felt that the visions were not from Hypatia. The crystals that she gathered were for her use in Agartha, because of her time as Hypatia's carer she already knew how to clean crystals but Hypatia was teaching her how to charge and programme the crystals. Hypatia explained that it was of extreme importance to learn about her crystals, their personalities, and their strengths. At times Timo, would doubt herself and need reassurance, even more so when she started to receive visions on her role in Agartha.

On one such night Timo had received a vision which upset her deeply. She was with her father and she was healing a pony, her father insisted that she use crystals to help with the healing; however, she felt that Ianthe's skills and knowledge of the herbs would be better suited for the task. While Timo felt that this approach was wrong, her father remained adamant, so she proceeded to use the crystals.

The pony died and she blamed herself, believing that she should have listened to her intuition. After that she refused to use crystals for healing, only using them for the power grid that surrounded and protected the city. She tried to carry on as if everything was OK, but she held a small amount of resentment towards her father. From that day forward their relationship was strained not only with her father but with all the appointed leaders of Agartha. He tried to repair the bond but she kept him at a distance. As a result, the harmony of the city began to suffer and she eventually left the city to live in solitude in the outskirts.

Timo woke up, shaking, and asked me if she would be able to speak to Hypatia.

"Hypatia has instructed me to allow you access to M's chamber," I said. "You will be in there alone. When you have finished, Hypatia will let you know when it is safe to leave."

Timo had never been alone with Hypatia, so this was an honour. "But, Gaia. I do not have a link with Hypatia."

"Timo, do not worry so, Hypatia has permitted you the gift of hearing, so you will be just fine."

Although permission was given to Timo she was very nervous to be alone with Hypatia; she took quite a while before she reached Hypatia's chamber, and as expected Hypatia was gentle in her approach towards Timo as she knew Timo's reasons for her nervousness.

"Timo, it pleases me that you seek my advice," Hypatia said. Timo however was not too graceful with her approach, not from a lack of trying but purely out of stored nervous energy, the statement just blurted out of her mouth without a single thought.

"Hypatia, am I truly the correct person to have this responsibility? In my vision, last night, I killed a horse. I fell out with my father, blaming him for the loss and I left the city." Timo now started to cry uncontrollably. Hypatia allowed her the time to release her pent-up emotions then proceeded to open a dialogue with Timo.

"Timo, you are the perfect person. You have proven yourself many times over to be a kind and gentle soul, who will do what it takes to be all that you can be. This vision is not a vision of what is going to happen, but a vision to show you what could happen if you doubt yourself. Only two days ago did you not wonder if Ianthe would be a better conduit for the crystals, but last night you discovered that you could talk to your labradorite and understand it. Furthermore, just so you know, that particular crystal chose you."

Timo just sat and listened but it was clear that she was in a more agreeable frame of mind.

"Your ascension in to what you are becoming was seen long before you were born. There will be times when you are in disagreement with your father, and again the vision was showing you to trust and use your intuition, which is one of the reasons why the labradorite came to you. He will help you to develop your abilities to become a very wise and powerful keeper of crystals."

After that day, the visions came thick and fast. She was now receiving guidance from all kinds of sources and, on occasion, had knowledge downloaded to her from sources not of this world.

Timo was expanding so fast that she was giving advice to me. The first time she did so, she stopped herself in mid-flow, "Oh, priestess, please forgive me. I forget myself."

I laughed: "Timo, if I felt you meant to disrespect me, you would not have got past the first word. You have grown to be a person that is worthy to give guidance and advice."

Timo had been back from her trip with Maeja for five months now, and I felt that she would only have weeks before it was time for her to leave.

As the days progressed, I found that I was spending less time with Timo. I had taught her all I could, and by now Maeja was just a bystander. Even Hypatia was beginning to relax with the amount of information that she was giving to Timo. Timo was now starting to get visions of the journey to her father and she also knew that the time was looming. Her chambers were now full of crystals of all shapes and sizes, and some of them needed two people to carry them; it was a situation that would often give us a cause for amusement, a fact that Timo would protest at, but as much as she protested we would not waste an opportunity. Eventually the time came when there was no good reason why Timo could not make her final transition; with the help of the crystals, she sent word to her newest friend, Trexus, requesting him to bring extra help. She informed him how many horses were needed and when to be ready. He in turn knew what was needed to be done.

On the morning of her departure, I came to Timo's chamber, where she was talking to Maeja. I stood in her doorway and watched in quiet contemplation at how much she had grown. *She has grown into quite a powerful woman,* I quietly thought, I should have known better.

"Yes," Hypatia said. "She is quite a woman. I will miss her dearly."

"As will I," I said with a tear in my eye, it was not a tear of sorrow but a tear that was full of pride for my friend. As I walked in to greet her, she hugged me firmly.

"Oh, Gaia," she said. "I will miss you so much." She was in floods of tears, which in turn gave me the need to release my own emotions.

"Make sure to visit," was all that I could bring myself to say, and then we both laughed as we cried.

"Humans are too emotional; what a waste of energy." Maeja said, disguising her true feelings and hiding them well. We both looked at each other and jumped on Maeja, wrestled her to the ground and proceeded to play with her.

Timo's chambers backed onto the gardens and I had instructed Hypatia to direct Trexus and his company to this area so that the horses could be loaded without too much hassle. When Trexus got to Timo's chamber and saw the amount that needed transportation, he backed away carefully trying not to make a sound from the room.

"And where do you think you are going?" I asked with humour in my voice.

"I fear I have brought the wrong companions," he said

in jest. "I brought my brothers and sisters, however, I should have asked if Abraxas had any relatives on this planet from his home world, or if he knew of anything bigger, like let's see an elephant." I almost wet myself with laughter, and at that point Timo entered the room.

"I heard that and I will treat it with the contempt that it deserves – and you can come out of there, Maeja, I can hear you sniggering." Maeja entered the room laughing.

"Trexus, you really hit the mark with that one," Maeja said.

"Timo, don't listen to them, they are only jealous."

Hypatia could not help herself, as always she was linked in to all that happened in Atlantis and the opportunity was too good to miss.

"Is that humour I hear in your voice, Hypatia?"

"Why no, my sweet child," she was now laughing. "So sorry, Timo, but it did look funny to me, to see this mighty horse back up out of fear." This line of banter continued for too long but the time did come when Timo had to leave.

All the festivities done with, and the horses packed, Timo was ready to leave. She went directly to the head priestess, and on entering her room Timo could not help but notice that Chrysanta was sitting patiently on her bed, with a small bundle of her possessions. In all the time that Timo spent at the temple she had never seen Chrysanta leave the temple, so was more than curious as to the reason why she looked the way she did.

"Head priestess, are you also leaving the temple on this day of all days, is Gaia sending you on a mission?"

"Hypatia felt that you needed my company and to also keep you in check."

Timo was ecstatic to hear the news, ran to her and squeezed her tremendously hard.

"Timo my dear, allow me to breathe."

"Oh Chrysanta, this news brings me so much joy."

"So it seems, as it did me when I was told."

"When did you know?"

"It came to me in my dreams last night, a gift from the great crystal."

Chrysanta was not the only person to receive visions in her sleep that night. There were a select number of people who had received instruction through visions to ready themselves for a journey and they all were told to wake and leave right there and then. Precise instructions as to the destination of their journey and the need for secrecy were given to them. They were instructed to be at the far side of the forest by early morning and travel in darkness until they reached their destination.

Trexus was well informed so knew where he was going, his connection to psychic awareness was gifted to him from birth, he was a special soul who was connected to higher realms and his connection was strong due to his family lineage. Because of this Timo did not have to have the knowledge of her destination, she was informed that Trexus had everything under his control so all Timo needed to do was sit and enjoy the ride. As they rode, Timo could hear voices in the distance, she clearly heard a voice saying, "They are here... ready yourselves, everybody," came a call in the distance.

Timo could now see a huge number of people in the distance, she turned to the head priestess: "Goddess, have all these people had visions as well?"

"It would seem so," Chrysanta replied, clearly shocked to see such a sight.

The crowd of people treated them like royalty for they knew that they were from the temple, even with the number of people that were now in the procession, the journey made good progress and they had reached their destination without difficulty and in good time.

On their arrival, Timo's father was waiting eagerly, Abraxas had told him that they were near and Silas could barely contain himself. However, he was taken back by the number of people that were with her. They greeted each other as if they had been apart for a long time, and then Timo introduced him to Chrysanta, while the people made camp, ate and rejoiced.

The following day, Timo and Chrysanta were taken to the path by Silas, who explained what it was and where it led. They then went back to the camp where instructions were left for the gathering of food for a long journey. Abraxas – up to this point – had kept himself away from the camp; his presence was not needed at that time, he waited by a pond, it was the place that he called home and was private to him and Silas.

"I want you to meet a friend of ours." Silas took Chrysanta by the hand and Timo was excited to see what Chrysanta would think of Abraxas. On rounding a huge tree and bush Chrysanta caught her first glimpse of Abraxas, Chrysanta stood with her mouth open in astonishment. Abraxas bowed in acknowledgement and allowed a link to be established: "Blessing to you, Chrysanta."

"Goddess, it spoke to me… it clearly spoke to me and it knows my name." It was most rude but understandable. Chrysanta was not one of the fortunate ones to have an animal link, so never grew up knowing the wonders that existed coupled with the fact that the only animals that she ever saw were linked to the temple, so to see this splendid specimen was most unexpected.

"My name is Abraxas; I am a he."

"P-p-p-pleased to meet you, and please forgive me."

Timo had never seen the head priestess stammer before, so along with her facial expression found this amusing. Timo went up to Abraxas and stroked his cheek.

"And how have you been? Has my father been boring you with his tales?" Timo used verbal communication as well as a telepathic link for the benefit of Chrysanta.

Once the formalities were over, Abraxas explained the situation:

"Ianthe will be here in two weeks. The Atlanteans are to be brought before me, and then I will take them some of the way to Agartha. Timo and Chrysanta, you will travel to the shore just beyond the rise to the north to meet them there, which will take you one day on horseback. Trexus knows of the place.

"Ianthe travels with people from Lemuria; Chrysanta, these people are not like Atlanteans. They have been oppressed and there is a high level of fear but they trust that the goddess has brought them to us. However, the hands of the temple have caused doubt with these people, and they need to see the fruits of their journey before they lose hope. Timo knows of these people and what has befallen them, listen to her she will tell you all that you need to know in the days that follow, before you depart to meet them. Silas, you know what is needed."

When the Atlanteans arrived at the site, Abraxas had chosen a spot that put him on the top of a small hill with the sun at his back. Timo and Chrysanta led the people towards Abraxas, whereupon seeing him, they stood back in fear.

"Where have you brought us? Is this a demon?" they cried out. At the sound of the word 'demon', Abraxas rose on his hind legs and stamped down with such force the earth shook. This got their attention and now they were quiet. At which point Silas came out from behind the tree.

"People of Atlantis, you know of me. I am Silas, healer of the animals, father to Timo and friend to all. This is Abraxas, and he has been friend to me for many years. He is as wise as he is old and he has been here watching over us for as long as our ancestors have walked this earth. You have been chosen from our people to form a new civilisation. You have all received the visions and know of the importance of this new beginning, so rise up now and let us travel to our new home."

Abraxas rubbed his head on Silas's shoulder to show the people he was, as Silas said, a friend – an act that nearly put Silas off balance. He then bent down and Silas mounted him. Now the people were in wonderment and they followed as directed.

Silas shouted back to Timo, "I will see you both in Agartha in a few weeks. Your things will be ready when you arrive."

The sight of her father riding Abraxas brought pride and admiration into Timo's heart, and if she could have smiled wider, her lips would have reached her ears.

"That was so amazing," Chrysanta commented. "Abraxas is a wonder that I never ever thought that I would see, I feel truly blessed."

"As do I, Chrysanta, as do I." The women went back to the camp where Trexus and six of his brothers were waiting to which Timo addressed him. "We will be ready when the time comes, Trexus, for now we will rest and talk, there are things that I need to prepare for Chrysanta. I will rely on you to keep me informed of Ianthe's approach and when the time is right for us to leave to meet them."

"He is truly a magnificent specimen, isn't he?" Trexus said.

"Yes he is. Tell me, Trexus, are those wings for show?"

"Why no, priestess, they have purpose as your father can testify."

"Wait no, he has flown with him?"

"He certainly has, and he was making quite a noise… woke up the whole forest." This brought much laughter to Timo and Chrysanta, eventually Timo started to explain all that she had learnt whilst in the company of Maeja and myself. Timo remembered it all and Chrysanta was amazed and wondered just how special would Timo become. With all that was being discussed the time soon came when Timo was informed that the time had come, the ladies broke camp and mounted their rides.

They arrived at the site and made camp. When Chrysanta awoke, she felt revitalized and had noticed that her life-force blood had started its cycle again; something that was unheard of for a woman of her mature age, as was fitting for people such as us it was not a subject that was needed to be discussed so she cleaned herself and made the necessary changes in how she wore her garments, on her return she was confronted by an ecstatic Timo.

"Oh, Chrysanta," Timo cried out, full of excitement.

"Come look… the ships."

"Sweet, goddess, how many people are there?" Chrysanta said. "We will need a city to house them all!"

"Maybe we should turn them away," Timo said in jest.

"Oh hush, child, it's just a passing comment." They both chuckled.

Timo could contain herself no longer and she ran to the water and dived in. "Priestess, you forget yourself." Timo was not listening; all that was on her mind was Ianthe. Her dearest sister was finally home. Timo worried so much about her safety, there were times when she wondered if she would ever see her again but now she was here. It seemed as if Ianthe had the same thoughts… even more so after the departure of Ourania. She could feel Timo's energy and no sooner did Timo go into the sea, Ianthe dived in, much to the surprise of the crew and all on board.

"Ianthe?" Petrus shouted out but she was gone. The girls swam good and hard and had to cover a vast distance, but to them there could be no distance great enough to keep them apart any longer.

When they were ready to get out of the water, Leonidas threw down some rope.

"Take hold, priestess," Leonidas shouted. "And who is this fair maiden?"

"This is my sister Timo," Ianthe said. "She is a priestess of Atlantis."

"Goddess, help us all, there are two of you!" The crew laughed as they pulled the two women on deck.

134

Chapter Seventeen

Ianthe

Ianthe was the last to enter the boat helped by Petrus. Even though Petrus had told her that this was the will of the goddess, Ianthe wanted to hear this from Ourania's lips herself. She was still clearly in distress and she didn't care who was watching, Ianthe was trained to serve Ourania. Between herself and Timo, the temple life and their place in it; was all she remembered. They had a place in the temple, a sense of belonging but now she was not in Atlantis, and Ourania was gone, in Ianthe's mind her life would not be complete with Ourania gone to what could only mean her certain death, the thought sent chills down her spine and just added to the pain that she was feeling. After a long painful time that was full of pleas and tears, Petrus finally got Ianthe on to the ship and into what was to become their cabin.

Early the following morning there was a lot of commotion on the deck. Bion went up top to see what the problem was and could see Leonidas, barking orders at his crew.

"Leonidas," Bion said, "what seems to be the problem?"

"Behind us, over there – look, there are a lot of ships on the horizon, do you suppose that the mad man has found you."

Bion's blood ran cold. "No, surely not! Not now with all that we have gone through, you must be wrong."

Ionas had come up on deck. He touched Bion's arm and as he did this Bion knew to link in with the earth-mother.

"Help me to understand, earth-mother," Bion said.

"These are your friends, Bion. They are the chosen ones who will join the others in Agartha." The answer came quickly, much to Bion's relief.

"Sweet goddess, be praised," he said, he then refocused his eyes and was surprised at what he was looking at.

"There are so many."

After the night's sleep Ianthe was more composed, with all that was happening on the deck, she could not help but to wonder what was going on, so she came up top with the others. She held Petrus's hand, turned and then looked into his eyes: "Will you be my strength now, Petrus?"

"If you will have me, I will be at your side until the end," he said.

"That would bring me great pleasure," she said, and then they kissed.

"Finally!" the brothers said, telepathically in unison.

The remainder of the voyage went without incident, and from the moment Ourania had left, Ianthe was getting stronger and stronger. Petrus and Bion assisted her when they could, but it seemed that her strength and wisdom had surpassed theirs, which they found astonishing. This however, unnerved the crew, who kept their distance at all times. However, Leonidas did have to ask her to not be so flamboyant in what she was doing. At Leonidas's request Ianthe took stock of the crew and all without exception was looking at her with a look in their eyes that caused Ianthe's heart to flutter with a feeling of deep shame.

"Oh, sweet goddess, what have I become? I have been so preoccupied in my thoughts that I have been blinded to your concerns. Please forgive me," she sobbed and then fell to her knees.

Petrus went to her but Leonidas stopped him, for he knew that task had to be one of his crew. The man that taunted them on their first voyage stepped forward. He placed his hand on her head and the feeling of his energy made her jump slightly.

"Ianthe, priestess, you have been through a lot of pain and I cannot even begin to imagine your loss. However, you must stop punishing yourself. I have seen this in my travels and this is not good for you, this will not end well.

We do not understand the ways of your people but we do know you all to be a kind and gentle people. Do not let Ourania's sacrifice become your burden."

Ianthe looked up at him, there was a small level of shock in her eyes for this man was not the most eloquent of souls so his words did not seem to fit the man. He helped Ianthe to stand, when she did she embraced him. "Thank you," she whispered in his ear, and gently kissed his cheek which caused him to blush with embarrassment. The rest of the crew offered their apologies for what Ianthe had to bear, and she thanked each one of them personally.

Peace had been restored on Leonidas's ship and he was most pleased. Later that evening Ianthe questioned Petrus on a matter that troubled her mind.

"Petrus, I must ask you, there is something that troubles me about what happened earlier today."

"Tell me, Ianthe, what troubles you?"

"When you sense energy is it purely the energy that emanates from a person in your vicinity, or do you feel all energy?"

"Generally it comes from people that I am in contact with, however there have been times when I have felt the energy of the earth-mother prior to speaking to her."

"OK, so tell me did you feel any energy this morning after Leonidas approached me?"

"I am afraid I did not, why do you ask?"

"I did feel an energy; it was not an energy that I recognised but it did have immense power, at the time I felt that the man that spoke to me was not in control of his words, it felt as though somebody else was speaking through him."

"I have heard of this although I have not witnessed this with my own eyes but if what you are saying holds true then I would suggest that we are and have been constantly watched and helped."

The conversation continued for many days not only with Petrus but with all the brothers and not forgetting Bion and at times Leonidas. The conversations were always uplifting, so much so that often the crew would forget themselves and take a seat to listen in on the discussions that were being had.

Three months had passed since they left the shores of Lemuria and they had made good time, it seemed that the goddess had smiled on them with calm seas and a favourable wind. Then suddenly a call came out from above.

"Leonidas, we have reached land," a cry came from a man on the highest mast. *Thank the goddess,* they all thought, at which point Bion stepped forward.

"Leonidas, do you trust the powers that have brought us together and kept us safe on this voyage?"

"Yes, the goddess has blessed us."

"Now I ask you to let her finish her work."

"What are you asking of me, Bion?"

"To put your faith in the powers that govern this world and allow the earth-mother to guide us to where she wishes us to be."

"You ask too much, Bion," Leonidas said. "I am a man of the sea. I understand her but you ask me to close my eyes to what I know and have faith in what I do not."

"Yes, that is exactly what I am asking."

Suddenly, Ourania's eagle, Liya, who had used the other ships to rest when she needed to, flew down to perch on Bion's shoulder. Ourania was always linked into Ianthe and Bion and knew what was needed, so sent Liya to them.

"Do you speak to the animal too, Bion?" Leonidas asked.

"Sadly no but Ianthe might be able to."

Liya flew to Ianthe and then Ianthe linked in with Hypatia: "Hypatia, tell me what you wish for me to hear."

"We have sent Liya to you, to guide you to where Timo and your father are waiting."

The sound of Timo and her father made her heart race with excitement. She cried aloud, "Oh, sweet goddess, thank you, thank you, thank you. Leonidas, follow Liya… she knows where to go."

Leonidas and Bion looked at each other, laughed, and said in unison: "Follow that bird."

"Follow Liya!" Leonidas bellowed. The crew followed his orders without questioning him.

They sailed for another two days before reaching their destination. Leonidas shouted for Ianthe: "Priestess, I feel we have arrived, the bird stops, priestess." Ianthe came up top and had a long look at the shoreline. She was unfamiliar with her surroundings and thought that they must be some distance from Atlantis.

"Sweet goddess," she cried and without any care or thought for her life, she dove into the sea.

"Timo," she had linked in with her sister and now they were racing towards each other.

Chapter Eighteen

Agartha

When all the ships were unloaded of their cargo and passengers, Timo and Ianthe took the captain aside.

"Leonidas what you have done for these people has not been unnoticed by the goddess. We have been instructed to give you this gift, you are to continue east until you reach a land that seems never to end, sail around this land until the morning sun is over the land. Find safe harbour and wait a full ten cycles before you set off to sail these waters again. There will be a period of five days when it will not be safe to sail, and once that time has passed, the place you know as Lemuria will be no more. You and your crew will never know hardship; the earth-mother will see to that as you are all family to her."

Leonidas thanked the ladies and made his departure leaving the remaining ships to the fate of the seas. Leonidas as always listened to the advice that was given to him by his new friends and they were true to their word.

Chrysanta was in awe at the number of people that were on the coast, she was now in a wonder as to just how big the place was that they were going to be inhabiting. The people were informed that time was pressing and there was still a journey ahead of them, so without delay the people gathered their things and were ready to be on their way. Bion and the others got on to the horses that had been provided for them, and they turned towards the road to Agartha. Bion was always aware that he would not be travelling to Agartha, so when the time came, he was not at all surprised to see his horse stop in its tracks.

Timo had spent most of the journey talking to Bion about Ourania. She knew her sister well and understood that her departure would have had a devastating effect on her, so didn't wish to bring up any painful memories.

When Bion's horse stopped, Timo asked him what seemed to be the problem.

"My horse does not wish to proceed with this part of our journey. I am sure that if you ask him he will tell you that this part of my journey is over and I am destined for a different path." He was correct and the horse confirmed that he was to wait there for Abraxas.

Ianthe had been keeping an eye on Timo, thinking that the bond between Timo and Bion was more than just newly acquainted friends. So, when she saw Bion stop then head in a different direction, she rode up to Timo to ask what was happening.

"Bion will not be with us in Agartha," was all that Timo said.

"Bion too, I should have guessed – there was always something about his demeanour that had me puzzled. Ourania hid hers well, but I don't think he was trying to hide what he knew, just keep it private," Ianthe called to Bion as she rode. Bion stopped his horse, Ianthe was now back on familiar ground, surrounded by close friends and family so was back to her true self and at her strongest, she proceeded to scold him.

"After all that we have gone through, you dare to sneak off without even a goodbye?"

"Oh, priestess," he said.

"It is Ianthe; it will always be Ianthe. I think you of all people have gained that right."

"Ianthe, I didn't wish to cause you any more distress… you have been through enough."

"And this is the perfect way to achieve that isn't it. Now come here and say goodbye like a true friend," Ianthe dismounted her ride so that she could say her farewells properly.

"You know it's quite a shame," Ianthe said. "I would have liked to have seen Gaia and Maeja one last time again in the flesh. I guess I should settle for their essence when we join."

"Goodbye, my sweet Ianthe. Be well."

141

"And you, Bion. May the goddess guide and strengthen your every step." With that there was nothing more to say, he mounted his horse and was on his way.

Timo re-joined her sister. "He is a very wise man," she said. "In the short time that I was with him, he opened my eyes to so much."

"Yes, he is. I thought that maybe there was a chance that he and Ourania might have gained more than friendship."

"He is a high priest. He will always be a high priest and he will never marry because his path is different to ours."

"But we are priestesses, so does that not mean the same can be said of us?"

Timo then explained what she had been told: "We will have companions and will bear children. You already have your companion and mine will come in time." Ianthe blushed.

"Oh, you thought I didn't know? I knew long before you set foot on these shores… we are still sisters but we just have different roles to play now."

"And what of Chrysanta?" Ianthe asked.

"She does not know it yet but she is to carry on our temple ways in Agartha."

"Oh, and who will be high priestess and high priest?"

"There will be no high priest," Timo said. "But she will be matriarch of the temple, a temple that she will be responsible for."

"Tell me, sister, when did you learn all of this?"

"Oh, Ianthe, we have both acquired knowledge that will seem strange to the other. That is the way it was supposed to be. I understand this fully now. We will be building a society that in time will be headed by you, father and I. We each bring one piece of equal share to the table and it seems that plans are in place for the brothers… it seems that they are an integral part of the plan for Agartha."

"Oh, goddess, in my excitement I forgot… where is father? Is he well? Why is he not here?"

"He is on his way to Agartha with the Atlanteans,"

Timo said.

"What is it like? Have you been there?"

"I have not, Ianthe, so on that point we are as one."

"Oh Timo it seems unbelievable that we will be with him again," Ianthe was excited at the prospect of being in the company of her father.

"Yes, I know, we are truly blessed. I thank Hypatia for giving us this responsibility."

"Do you know where it is where we are going?"

"No, I have been told that Trexus knows of the location. We are in his care."

At that point, Trexus came to a halt. "Priestess, we are at the meeting point where we will wait for Abraxas."

"Wait!" Ianthe said. "Abraxas the mythical horse that father would tell the most wondrous stories about?"

"Yes, the very same, and let me tell you, the stories do not compare when you stand next to him."

"You have seen him?"

"I have met him and he is truly glorious."

The girls dismounted and helped the others to get comfortable, as they didn't know how long they would be there for.

Abraxas had arrived at Agartha and had given some trustworthy people instructions. He took Silas with him via the top of the volcano; he knew that the Lemurians had arrived at the designated place and would soon get restless. With great haste he left the Atlanteans to go directly to the Lemurian camp, he circled the encampment before he came in to land. When he was spotted, a loud scream was heard in the distance closely followed by another and then another, and soon the whole camp was in a panic: "A demon."

"No wonder I looked for solitude away from ignorant people," Abraxas said to Silas. "Some things will never change."

Ianthe was in awe.

"He is magnificent." Then she fell to her knees. "Is that father? Oh, it is, it must be," she said sobbing.

"Oh, Father," Timo called out to him. "You know how to make an entrance."

"Abraxas is to blame. Now, come and greet me, my beautiful daughters?"

Ianthe was trying desperately hard to dry her tears behind Timo, as she did not wish for him to see her like this.

"Oh, sweet goddess, is that her, the little child that I sent off to become a woman? What is with those tears? Come to me, my child, I have seen you in worse shape than that."

The three hugged until Abraxas broke up the reunion. "Ianthe, it is an honour to finally meet you," he said. "Your father speaks of you dearly."

"Thank you, Abraxas, I too have heard of you, and the honour is all mine."

"We must leave, as the journey is far and I have business elsewhere."

"Are we expecting more people?" Ianthe asked.

"No, my business is closer to home. That is all that I will say. I will travel with you to the outskirts of Agartha then I will leave you in your father's care." When they did reach the cavern, Abraxas left to join Bion.

Bion was sat on a rock, the horse that he was riding had come to a stop as soon as he knew that the travellers were on their way. Bion had no idea why they had stopped, but took the opportunity to take care of some much-needed personal business.

***

Two weeks had passed since Bion had separated from the group, with no contact from Demeta and now he was getting anxious. *Is it because I am in a strange land?* he thought. The voyage had taken its toll and he would drift off to sleep quite frequently. The day that he was to meet Abraxas he was in a deep slumber and awoke to discover a giant horse with wings standing over him.

"What manner of beast are you?" Bion exclaimed, not realising that not only his words but his thoughts could be heard by Abraxas.

"Good evening to you, sir, we have not had the pleasure of meeting, Bion. I, however, have you at a disadvantage for I know you well. As for me my name is Abraxas, friend to Hypatia, Timo, Ianthe and the earth-mother."

Bion said nothing. *Is this horse – well I think it's a horse – talking to me?* he wondered.

"Yes, I am Bion," sounding more serious. "I have gifted you with the power to communicate with animals, the horse is a distant cousin to me, so let's not get ourselves confused."

"Are there more like you here? In all the time that I spent with Ourania, she never hinted that such creatures live here."

"Not like me, yet plenty of other animals live here."

Now Bion felt foolish. "My apologies, Abraxas."

Abraxas knew full well what questions troubled Bion's mind and without being asked, sought to answer some of the more important ones.

"Earth-mother sends her apologies; we are aware that you have questioned your link to her but she wanted you to meet with me before she communed with you in this land. Now heed what I have to say, Bion, I will give you instructions on this place to help you adjust and to prepare you for your people. There is much to share, so I suggest that you sit back down and listen very carefully."

Abraxas went through a long list of do's and don'ts, he finished telling Bion about the animals, by saying: "Respect them and they will respect you. Demeta has looked into the souls of all who are coming from your homeland to these shores, and those she deemed to be trustworthy have been sent here through visions. This was designed to facilitate you becoming the next high priest and the last true high priest of Atlantis, just as it was in your dream."

Now Bion was impressed: *He could see my dream,* he thought, forgetting that Abraxas could hear his thoughts.

"Yes, your dreams as well as the essence of your soul, the life you had and the life you are to have."

"Telepathic communication, I forgot," he said aloud.

"Yes, and you would do well to remember that in Lemuria, there are those who can sense energy, whereas we can see thoughts."

"See thoughts?" Bion said. "Surely, you mean hear thoughts."

"I say what I mean to say. Bion, make no mistake I need to prepare you for the Atlantean people, but more so for Gaia and Maeja, as they can be a handful if you are not ready for them. Now with all of that taken care of, I must go to Agartha while you rest, as you will have a busy day tomorrow. I will be back to check in on you later."

***

The path to Agartha was full of natural traps and perilous falls. The new arrivals were weary and apprehensive in the direction that this journey was heading in, this part of their destination was not revealed to them. The same could be said about the Atlanteans, so now that they were moving through the earth and going deeper into the body of the earth, it gave all a small sense of fear. The only aiding factor was the fact that these people were more in tune with the earth-mother. As the guiding principle that these people lived by was in fact the earth-mother, they could feel her love getting stronger as they got deeper into her body.

Eventually they reached their destination, there was one man to greet them at the opening to the cave. Timo and Ianthe were dumbstruck at the sheer size of what they were now looking at:

"And to think I was worried that all these people would not fit in here comfortably?" And now Chrysanta was feeling a little foolish. "I should have known that Hypatia would not make any miscalculations."

The man that was waiting at the entrance was one of the priests from the temple. He greeted Chrysanta in their customary manner. Petrus, being the only one of the brothers who could speak asked the obvious question:

"But where are all the Atlanteans? I was led to believe that there was a large Atlantean presence."

"This cave is a lot bigger than it seems; look over in that far north-western area. Do you see it?" The man pointed out the area that the Atlanteans had been taken to.

Petrus began to make out movement, "Yes, I believe I do, goddess. This place must be three times the size of Lemuria."

It took a further two hours to reach the Atlanteans. By the time they reached their destination, Abraxas had returned and he summoned all to come to him.

When all were gathered, Abraxas opened a link so that all could hear and understand the importance of what this place was, and what it represented. Now he addressed the people: "Atlanteans, Lemurians. You are now one people; one race with one common goal, the preservation of life and love. Lemurians know and understand what can happen if this is lost, and those from Atlantis know what it means to live in harmony with each other. These people who have brought you here have been selected and personally trained and guided by the great crystal and earth-mother. They will be your leaders, matriarchs, advisers, healers and keepers of the knowledge of what will be lost in times to come on the surface." As Abraxas was giving his instructions, he singled out Silas, Timo, Ianthe, Petrus, Ionas, Kallias, Miltiades and Chrysanta.

"Follow them, listen and ask them for help, but do not stray from the path that has been set out for you, for you are the chosen few and in this place, you will be judged if you flout with the laws of this sacred place. You are in the heart of the earth-mother and she will provide for all your needs so that you may flourish. Even your leaders will not be able to stop Demeta's wrath if you disappoint her, for she has put a lot of faith in your hands, as have we all. Live well, live long and live happy. Now witness the power of the galactic command of mother-earth, of the great crystal and of me." He turned to Silas: "Are you ready, my friend?"

"Ready for what?" Silas asked.

"The promise of a gift, you will not lose control but the transference will be the same as before." Silas remembered the bears holding him and he being asleep for days. "OK, I trust you, do what you must."

Abraxas tilted his head down and now his horn was glowing. He gently touched Silas's forehead; Silas could instantly feel his skin tightening, the numbing ache in his bones disappearing, the sight in his eyes get clearer, and his whole being was so full of energy. He looked at his daughters and their faces was confirmation that a transformation had taken place, Silas's age had been reversed from sixty-five, to a healthy thirty-five-year-old man. Abraxas then told the others to come close and join hands.

"This gift that I have bestowed on Silas, I now gift to you all, and to ensure that the plan for Agartha keeps on the path that the creator has set out for it, I give to you all a gift of longevity, for you are the guardians of this new beginning. Now this is your domain, so guard it well."

This small group were now all in their thirties. The brothers regained the use of their tongues and the whole group of chosen ones shared a link with each other.

Now Abraxas had a private audience with each of the chosen, he checked to see that they had bonded well to all that was given to them and when he was finished he gathered them all together for a final farewell. "My work here is now done," he said. "I go now to join my old friend and help with the preparation of Atlantis." He stretched his wings and then flew off.

That evening Abraxas arrived at Bion's camp and needed to express the importance of the animal kingdom to Bion. What started out to be a gentle lesson soon grew out of control. During the night whilst Bion was well asleep Abraxas went into the forest and gathered up some of his larger friends, two of which were white tigers by the name of Petra and Callas. Abraxas explained to his friends what he was looking to do but a bear in this small group started to chuckle; all the animals of this land knew of Abraxas's humour, so when the question was asked as to the reason for his humour, the bear expressed the wish to have fun with the unsuspecting man. All in the group looked at Abraxas with a pleading look and he felt obliged to allow the wish to stand. That morning Bion could feel a roughness running across his cheek and it was wet with an odour of what could only be described as death. He opened his eyes to be greeted by a huge tiger licking his face, Bion froze; he could feel his legs were pinned down, he angled his head to discover that there was another tiger on his lower body. Bion let out an almighty scream, his life was over. As he did, Abraxas came out from behind a bush, trying desperately to contain himself.

"This is an important lesson for you to learn, my friend," Abraxas tried to sound serious.

"Don't you dare call me friend," Bion jested but the level of fear was still evident. "I have never been so scared in my life."

"Good, then the lesson was well received, like I explained yesterday, these are wild territories and the laws here are different to city laws. It will serve you well never to forget this, I have instructed these two tigers to stay with you until your people arrive, after that you will be on your own. Do not forget what you have learnt here this past day and teach your people, teach them well. I will leave you now as I have business in Atlantis." Once again Abraxas was gone as quickly as he came.

Chapter Nineteen

Reconnection

Nearly two years had passed from leaving her companions on the shore, before Ourania made her entry into the city. She had spent her time meditating and gaining the strength and courage that she would need for this her final days on the planet. In her meditations, she kept a constant check on Ianthe's journey via Hypatia, so knew that she had reached Agartha. So now that she was satisfied that all was in place, Ourania made her advance to the outskirts of the city. Ourania planned her arrival for high night, as she approached the city walls she witnessed a flood of people leaving the city. She did not need to ask why they were leaving in such a hurry, Ourania was sure she knew the reason why. That was confirmation enough that she was on her final journey. Try as she might, Ianthe's outburst still haunted her, she knew that for her to succeed with what she had to do she had to put Ianthe's outburst out of her mind, Petrus had explained that Ionas had left word with a friend to help Ourania with whatever she wanted. However, this person had been discovered just prior to Ourania's arrival; Hypatia warned Ourania that this person's light had been extinguished by the priest, news that did not surprise Ourania at all, Hypatia asked one more time just to be sure if Ourania wanted to continue on this path. The answer did not change, neither did the conviction of the answer. With that established Ourania was updated as to what was waiting for her, from that moment on she was prepared for whatever came her way. However, before she had a chance to go through the gates of the city, her arm was grabbed from behind. "Follow me," the voice said to her.

"Who are you?" Ourania asked. She was clearly shaken.

"Ionas sent me. We must leave this place. You are in danger." At that point, some guards rushed past them and a priest was pointing out people who were being seized by the guards.

"What is this?"

"Word of the migration has reached the priest and he is trying to find out where they were going. All those who have been detained and questioned have no idea." Ourania knew why, but she also knew this man was not who he claimed to be. *Perfect*, she thought, *all is going to plan.*

With the help of her guide, Ourania worked her way through the city being careful to keep her energies low. She had learnt a lot from Bion and she was quite skilled at masking her energy. They had left some large streets, went down some back streets, and then entered the house of a merchant. "You must be Ourania. I am Irenius, and I will be here to help you with your needs."

"You are not from this place," Ourania said. "I detect that your energy has a different signature to the others."

Ourania knew full well that there was nobody here that Petrus and the brothers trusted.

"They said that you are very perceptive, I am impressed. I am from the city of Hierapolis... a place far from here."

"Do you have a place that I can rest?" Ourania asked. "I have been travelling for quite some time and need to gather my thoughts?"

"Why yes of course," he said. "Just through here."

She was taken to a back room where she was able to rest, but instead, she linked in with Hypatia.

"Hello, my friend," Ourania said. "I have found the man that we were seeking. His energy matches what you transmitted."

"I promise you, Ourania, your sacrifice will not be in vain."

Only Demeta and Hypatia knew the true level of Ourania's sacrifice and what she would have to endure.

The time came a lot quicker than expected. Ourania

was lying on the bed awake when some guards entered the room accompanied by the merchant. "You're not really a merchant, are you?" Ourania asked.

"No, I am not, but in time we will see what and who you truly are."

Ourania was taken to the mad priest, Hypatia and Demeta would remain at her side until the end.

"Be strong, my child. Thank you and may the love of the mother be with you always."

In the cave, Ianthe could feel Ourania. She let out a chilling scream to which Petrus came running over. "What troubles you, my love?"

"It's Ourania. She has been taken by the priest." They both knew that it would be just a matter of time before he started to work on her; Ianthe sought to link in with Hypatia, and due to the link that the guardians of Agartha now shared all the guardians were now together to support Ianthe.

In Atlantis, Maeja felt it first but there was no mistaking the energy signature. She ran to me and I was already on my way to M's chamber.

"What is the meaning of this? This is not the path I was shown in the vision," I demanded, too upset to remember my place.

"Be careful of your thoughts, Gaia. Your emotions betray you... that vision had to be changed."

"Why?" I demanded.

"As you know, Gaia, there are many forks in a road and there are times when a new road needs to be travelled to achieve the desired destination. We of the Command have long understood that the only thing that is constant throughout the entire multiverse, is this simple fact. Nothing remains constant, one of the most basic laws in the multiverse."

"Is Ourania held as a prisoner to the very man that they were trying to avoid?" I asked again, allowing my emotions to rule over my thoughts and actions.

"She is, Gaia, but she did this on her own judgment

after consulting with Demeta and me."

"Why was I not consulted on this matter?"

"For this very reason, Gaia," Hypatia said. "You need to control your energy. Do not lose yourself here."

I was now crying, more out of frustration and the need to help my mentor and friend in her hour of need.

"You knew this day would come, Gaia, so calm yourself. This is what Ourania wanted. She planned this and forced me to keep the finer details from you."

"Ourania forced you..." I said. "Since when does anybody force you?" My emotions where still running high.

Hypatia knew that I loved Ourania like a mother and this would be a hard lesson to bear.

"When a person has a compelling argument," she said. "When what they are requesting is for the benefit of all and not the self; when they hold all the cards and use them for leverage; and when it is justified, that's when."

That sounds like Ourania... and as usual, Hypatia has made her case, I thought. I could feel Maeja's concern; she had stayed quiet throughout the entire communication, as she knew that her input would not help. She only wished that I would stop hurting myself with questions that I knew the answers to.

"Please, Hypatia, don't allow her to suffer."

"I promise you, Gaia, as soon as we have what we need, Ourania will join the galactic command and she will not suffer."

Timo, Ianthe and Petrus then linked in with us. They were as emotional as I was and were demanding answers:

"I have to put a stop to this now."

Hypatia was not happy and she clearly wanted to take control of this situation, she did not wish for this to escalate any further.

"All that we have prepared rests with Ourania," Hypatia continued. "She is the bravest soul I have encountered in my time here. She put forward this plan when we knew that there was a force trying to steal

153

dangerous knowledge that would have destroyed the planet. I will not let her sacrifice be in vain, and although I know you all care very deeply about her wellbeing, you are not helping. If you wish to help her, build up your energy and help us locate the head of the snake."

"We are here to serve as always," I said. "Forgive us, we know that you have the interests of the planet at heart, and we are so emotionally attached to Ourania that we fail to see the big picture."

"I knew if I was stern with you, you would see sense," Hypatia said. "Now you sound like the high priestess. This is an important lesson for you all, detachment is a tool that will serve you well in this situation."

"Don't push it, Hypatia. I am still mad at you."

"Save that attitude, you are going to need it for the elders."

"Who are they?" Timo asked.

"We picked up their energy signature over fifty years ago, and then suddenly they vanished. We knew then that time was limited and they posed a serious threat to us all."

"Here in Agartha we have felt an energy that is strange to us. This energy has made Timo concerned, but more importantly who could shield themselves against you?" Ianthe said.

"That's what we have been working on," Hypatia replied. "And we got a small read on them twenty-plus years ago when they made a mistake. But they recovered quickly."

"Does this have something to do with Kaius?" Now Timo joined the conversation.

"It has a lot to do with him. It would seem that he was high up in their chain of command, and then he did something that made him a target and gave us a window."

Petrus felt that he could help in this matter so without hesitation he joined the conversation.

"We heard of a group of ex-communicated priests that came to Lemuria quite some time ago in the search of power and knowledge, it was said that they came from

Atlantis, yet that was before my lifetime and many years have passed since these priests were known to be in the city."

"Yes, I remember a group of priests led by one called Aaron," Hypatia interjected and now we could all feel her energy rising. "They were looking to take over from the high priestess at the time but the high priest threw them out of the order. I kept an eye on them as far as the edge of Atlantis, and then lost them after they crossed the water." Again, Petrus took over.

"But that was well over a hundred years ago... maybe even more if my knowledge serves me correctly."

"Yes it was... we have had three high priests since that time. So maybe it is the wrong thread. Furthermore, the energy that I first picked up on did not have an Atlantean signature."

Now Petrus was in full flow and the others just sat back and tried to keep up with the flow of conversation as it was now bouncing back and forth between Petrus and Hypatia.

"Is it not possible," Petrus said, "that they could have mixed it with Lemurian energy? And what if they didn't stop there. The story goes that they surpassed the priests of Lemuria and went east looking for more power!"

"That would have taken them to darker shores where dark arts are studied. Demeta, are you linked in?"

"Yes, Hypatia. I have been listening. I know of a group of travellers; who having gained such knowledge and power, had little respect for life, the earth or each other. Most of them were killed; however, six of them went to see a particular dark-minded practitioner, known as the collector where they lost their lives."

Petrus re-joined the conversation: "I have heard of this person. It is reported that he is over three hundred years old and that he has gained the ability to grant long life for a price. It is said that he made a pact with a dark ancient source that allowed him immortality if he collected souls for him... hence the name."

"Petrus, how sure are you of this?"

"My source was a man that I know to be ninety-five years old, yet he doesn't look a day over fifty. He claims to have met this man, for the price of his soul. Why does this bear any relevance?"

"That would explain a lot, Demeta. Is there anything you can do to verify this?" Hypatia said.

"I will try, but to delve into this matter will bring a great risk to us all."

Hypatia knew of the risk but she had to be sure. "If what Petrus is saying is true then that would explain why I have had difficulty tracing the energy."

"How can that be so?" Ianthe asked.

"Energy is connected to the soul," Hypatia said. "If the soul is pure, the energy is pure and strong; if the soul is un-pure, the energy is weak. So, if there is no soul, do you see how this works...? Demeta, before you do anything, let me check something out. Stay linked to my energy as I may have need of your help."

Hypatia was gone for only a few seconds and directed her energy to the last place that the energy vanished and was surprised to see a rock formation that did not stand true for the area.

"Demeta, do you see that?"

"Yes I do, Hypatia, and I can tell you it is not my work. It certainly is not natural; also, I am picking up a foul dirty energy that is making me feel quite ill."

"We must go now!" Hypatia said anxiously.

Hypatia was back. "This meeting is closed," she said. With that, she closed off communications with everybody except me.

"Gaia, I am in need of your assistance." There was something in Hypatia's voice that compelled me to listen quietly. Eventually, Hypatia spoke: "I have spoken to Abraxas and he is to fly you to Agartha. Do not ask him to divulge your mission... do you understand?"

"Yes, I do but..."

"No, child, no buts. Go, go now."

I had never seen Hypatia like this; now I was worried,

but took heed of her directness. Abraxas had arrived in Atlantis weeks earlier and I was mesmerised by his magnificence.

On leaving M's chamber, I went directly to the edge of the forest where Abraxas was waiting for me. I was thankful when he stooped down so I could climb up on him and in an instant, we were up and into the sky, before finally descending on the mouth of the volcano.

Silas felt his friend arrive and greeted him: "My friend…" was all he got to say.

"Where are the girls?" Abraxas asked rather abruptly, it was rude and he knew it but he had no time for politeness.

"On the southern wall," Abraxas did not wait for any further directions, he was off to find Timo and Ianthe.

"Do you have it?" he asked. Demeta had told the girls that they had to go with Petrus to the southern wall and retrieve a crystal that she was bringing to the surface.

"Yes." They handed over a large, heavy sack. He did not thank them or stop to form any conversation, he was off again straight back to Atlantis. Now he flew directly to M's chamber. Abraxas was no stranger to the chamber, in days past he was a frequent visitor to the chamber when the matriarch established the temple and the first high Priestess, he even had his own entrance, which I was surprised to see but grateful for, as holding onto that sack took all my strength.

"Open the bag, Gaia."

"What is it?" I asked but got no response, Maeja was sitting quietly through the whole exchange, but now she was taking notice of what was happening. Her ears pricked up and when I looked at her, her headpiece was glowing. I looked at my bracelet and it was glowing too. I turned to Abraxas and noticed his horn was glowing, and to my surprise, Hypatia took corporeal form and she was also glowing. The crystal began to rise out of the sack; as it rose, a strand of light stretched out to connect with all the crystals that were in this chamber and finally to Abraxas's horn, now it too was glowing, and before I realised it,

Abraxas, Maeja and I were levitating. No sooner did I realize this when the light that was coming from the crystal began to get brighter; this triggered the same from all the crystals as well as Abraxas's horn. Eventually the light became so intense, totally filling the chamber, that I was forced to close my eyes the light was that bright. The whole experience lasted ten minutes with no pause. When it was finished, I had to sit down, I was exhausted. Abraxas was the first to speak.

"She is all that you said she was, she will do just fine."

That was very cryptic, I thought, but I was too exhausted to question him.

Now Hypatia felt that she was free to explain and allowed the link to Agartha to be re-opened.

"Thank you all. When Petrus put me on the correct road, I went to where I lost the energy and what I found was so un-pure that it could only mean one thing. Demeta confirmed this for me by the fact that it made her feel ill. Only pure dark energy can do that to her, therefore, I knew if the forces behind that energy felt my presence, they would be able to infiltrate my energy field. That golden crystal is the heart-stone of this planet; it is one of the strongest, and the most precious gem on this world. Every world has one; it is the pure energy of the creator. There was a world that we tried to help once but were unable to. The heart crystal of that planet splintered into pieces; each piece was gifted by the creator to special souls, these souls would be able to activate the power within. Abraxas is the only living being with a piece forged into his physical being. My crystalline form was grafted around a large splinter, the mother if you like, while some of the remaining pieces have been crafted into jewellery to disguise their true nature. You and Maeja have one in your bracelet and headpiece. A piece was melded into Abraxas's horn as a gift to him by the creator for helping not only this world but many others. Timo, you know has one, and so too does Ianthe. There is one other who has one."

"Ourania," Maeja and I said together.

"Yes Ourania, she is with us now in the galactic command."

"They killed her," a chill went down my spine as I said the words.

"No, they didn't get the chance. Thanks to Petrus, she did not have to go through with what was planned, so we removed her from that plane of existence."

"So what about the threat to Atlantis?" I asked.

"The threat to Atlantis still remains, but not through the hands of the elders."

"What has happened to the elders?"

"They have been cleansed."

"Do you mean that we killed them?"

My questions were out of character for who I was but I was so frustrated with the whole situation that I had momentarily forgot my training and the vast amount of knowledge that I had stored within me.

"No, well not exactly, we put back what was taken."

"Which was what exactly?"

"Their souls."

"So how does that help Atlantis?"

Thankfully it was Ianthe who asked that question.

"The body cannot live without a soul, it violates the natural order of things, and putting the soul back into the body returns the body back to its natural state."

"But surely that is the last thing we want?" Again, Ianthe put the question forward as she was also angered at the departure of her friend and teacher.

"No, that is exactly what was needed. Putting the soul back into the body gave the body what it needed. A body should not live past its agreed time; the only source with the power to extend life is the same power that created it. As a result, the soul never leaves that body so the body does not miss it. When an unnatural interference takes place, like removal of the soul to extend life, that unnatural state can be corrected through the love of the creator – we call it blending. The balance is restored, leaving the body to revert back to its natural state."

"Yet you say that this is what we want, are we missing something here or is it just me that finds this irrational?" I could not remain quiet any longer.

"Gaia, you are not mad." There was a little hint of humour in Hypatia's voice for good reason. "If you allow me to finish, all will become clear. The natural state of the elders was for them to die nearly two hundred years ago. So now, they have simply returned to their natural state. The natural order of things is now in balance."

"So now they have passed on?"

"Exactly," Hypatia said. "We did not kill them; we returned them to their natural timeline."

"And what of Ourania?" Ianthe had to ask.

"She did not have to suffer as she had agreed to, so we honoured our promise to her."

"Could you not have rescued her?"

"Why would we rescue her when she has fulfilled the agreement that was made between her and the creator. We have honoured her contract and she is in her rightful place, as will you all be when the time comes."

"Then please help me understand why she even needed to be there?" Ianthe was clearly still emotional about the whole affair and not afraid to show it.

"We all felt that the connection to the acquisition of my source of power was Lemuria, we thought the link was Kaius. We thought that he had somehow linked with the priest there who made Lemuria what it is now. When Kaius passed over, we hoped that Ourania's fate had changed but alas, the threat remained. Ourania felt she had no choice but to proceed on to Lemuria and directly connect us to the mad priest; only then would we be able to stem this acquisition. Thankfully, Petrus provided us with the missing piece of the puzzle. Due to the level of shielding that these souls produced and the fact that we could not feel their souls, we had no option but to see this through."

"So what has happened to her?" I asked.

"You will see and you will understand, but please trust me and ask no more on this matter, Gaia, we know this has been a very troubling time for all of you, but I promise you that all will be revealed in time."

I recollected my thoughts and went to my chamber. Maeja as always was close by and concerned as my energy was not as it should be, but allowed me the privacy of my space and thoughts. I felt ashamed of my actions and now confused as I had allowed my emotions to get the better of me. Maeja could feel this very deeply and could stay silent no longer.

"Gaia, I have been with you all of your life. I have helped you and guided you in times when you have needed it. I have protected you from yourself as well as others and shared your pain, never asking for anything back in return. Now, I need to ask you to do something for me."

I put Maeja's head in my hands.

"You have been my rock, my pillar of strength, and my guiding light. Ask it of me and I shall do it."

"The time is fast coming when you must be stronger than you have ever been before," she said. "We should have a single mind. We cannot be at odds with Hypatia ever again... no matter who is suffering in pain, or even worse. In short, you must maintain your discipline. You were chosen for a reason, Gaia. Know that reason to be true and don't lose sight of our purpose for we both know that it is bigger than this plane of existence. You are better than that scared child I saw in M's chamber on your renaming day, and yes, there was a small element of fear in you. But just for the record, you have nothing to be ashamed of. You have showed your love for Ourania and that is something to be proud of. It took strength and courage to stand up to Hypatia the way you did for the safety of your friend, and if you are not proud of that fact, I tell you now that I am."

That night I was to get confirmation of this fact from Hypatia, who assured me that she held no grudge.

"Gaia, do I have permission to enter your space?"

"Oh, Hypatia, please do," I said. "Hypatia, I love you so much. Please forgive me for my irrational behaviour."

"This is the reason why I have come to you, Gaia. I cannot and will not forgive you."

My heart sank. *I have crossed the line and I will be cut off from what is to come,* a thought misplaced but it was there. *I may as well leave this work to Hypatia, Abraxas and Demeta; after all, do they really need me?*

"Have you quite finished, young lady? As I was going to say before you sealed your own fate, a fact that I would never do. I will tell you this though, young lady, I will never forgive you as I have nothing to forgive you for. Gaia, you have strength and love in abundance, and this is your driving force. Yes, you can be a bit headstrong but I would not change a thing or have you any other way. I love you dearly, Gaia, and will not try to change you. If I feel that you have crossed the line, I will tell you so, as I have on numerous occasions. Remember, Gaia... knowledge, wisdom, reason and feeling. These are the principles that guide my hand and, in time, they will guide yours too. Now, come to my chamber, I have something for you."

Maeja and Abraxas were in the chamber waiting for me when I arrived. "I have an audience," I said, surprised to see them there. Hypatia then explained the reason why they were there.

"Abraxas felt that this was important enough to share with you two but only you two." No sooner was that said when the walls went translucent and a vision formed. It was Ourania; she was standing with some extremely large entities that had a luminous glow about them but what was important here was I could feel the love, it was so pure, so fulfilling, so nurturing, it was the most beautiful expression of love that I had ever felt, so much so that I had to ask.

"I know this is love that I am feeling but I have never felt it like this before. I have felt Hypatia, and I have felt

Abraxas and Demeta, even Ourania but this – this is different; this is strong, pure, alive."

Then I stopped and burst out in tears as the realisation hit me.

"This is the love of the creator." Nothing more was said, they just allowed me to bathe in the creator's love. They left me there until I was ready to leave.

Chapter Twenty

Lost and Found

Word had come of refugees coming to Atlantis from a distant land; the word had travelled fast, mainly helped by some well-placed visions to all the correct people, to be finished quite appropriately by me addressing the people of Atlantis of the pending arrival of their distant cousins who needed shelter. The stage was set, the people busied themselves cleaning empty houses, clearing abandoned lands and finding areas of land that could be utilised for building new dwellings if needed. There was a positive flow of excitement in the city which fuelled the Atlanteans on with much haste.

The Lemurians had travelled for many weeks, away from the oppression of what their city had become. They were following a vision, that was gifted to them, as they slept the night before their departure; this guided them to a lone priest. His name was Zosimos, and one of Bion's closest friends. When Bion fled the city, Zosimos was the first to be taken. He was held until it was clear that he did not know of Bion's location, unlike some of the less fortunate priests, he was banished. This was done in the hope that Bion would try to contact him, but over the years it was to become clear that it was not the case. Eventually the mad priest became tired of the waiting game and brought back his spies.

Zosimos wandered the land for many years thereafter. Bion had heard of his capture but not his release, so feared that he had passed on, but Demeta had plans for this lone priest and kept his fate blinded to Bion's eyes. With the aid of visions from Demeta, Zosimos was guided to docks far from the city and to a captain who would be willing to take on a voyage, he even accepted a promise that payment would be made on the arrival of the remaining passengers and that the location would be revealed when sails were set. It was also suggested that more ships would be needed, and if the captain could procure them, then he would be paid handsomely for his service. The captain was a popular man, so this task was of little effort for him.

When people started arriving at the dock, Zosimos informed his captain that it was time. The captain took payment for the voyage and they set sail. The captain was happy to discover that his friend had left the dock to collect passage, only three weeks earlier for the lands of Atlantis. With a good wind behind them they may even be able to join his friend for the voyage but this was never the plan, they arrived one week after Bion's crossing a little further east but closer to Bion's location.

Having arrived at their location, they set camp. Zosimos was now in a state of mild panic, there was a high percentage of people who knew him from the temple and knew of his kindness and his friendship to the true high priest, those that did not know him were soon informed. This situation elevated Zosimos to becoming the chosen leader for this expedition. Before Zosimos put himself down to sleep, he quietly asked Demeta for a sign that would help him get his people to the city of Atlantis, his request was soon to be answered. During the night, Trexus came to Zosimos and nudged him while he was asleep. "Hello." Zosimos did not have the gift of talking to animals, but that didn't stop him from being polite. He stood up to greet his new friend and Trexus nudged him forward towards the tree line. Zosimos was no fool, and he instinctively knew that this was the sign he was waiting for.

"Thank you, my friend. I understand."

Morning broke and Zosimos declared that he had received a message in the night and the way was made clear to him. The group gathered their things and followed Zosimos, who occasionally would spot the horse, which kept him on track.

They walked for five days and rested at night.

Occasionally, Zosimos would get concerned as he lost his guide a few times but when he started to feel desperate, Trexus would appear again.

One of the days when walking, Zosimos heard a noise that startled him. He then noticed in the tree line a figure that had him extremely concerned. It was a tiger, and he knew the group was not equipped to meet such a formidable animal. Zosimos changed their direction in the hope that it was not interested in them. "Zosimos, come here quickly," came a cry from one of the travellers. At first glance, it appeared that the tiger's lunch had been interrupted. Bion was discovered asleep under a bush and one man had recognised him.

"Goddess be praised, our journey has been blessed... surely we will find the land of our vision, for they have sent back to us our high priest," cried the man that found him. All was as planned, Hypatia and I were pleased. The whole affair had been carefully engineered to help Bion get assimilated into Atlantis, but more importantly, into the temple. When Bion was fully awake he began to recognise people and he was more than surprised to see Zosimos standing in front of him.

"Zosimos, my friend. I feared you were butchered at the hands of that mad man. Oh, just to see you here brings me great joy." They hugged, laughed, cried and then they sat and talked. Zosimos noticed another tiger bigger than the first that he had seen, so suggested that they continued their discussion while they walked. They continued their journey for half of the day, then stopped to eat and rest when Zosimos noticed the tigers again.

"Bion, those tigers seem to be stalking us."

"No, not stalking us," Bion said laughing. "They are my friends. They feel obliged to stay with us until we reach Atlantis."

Bion looked to see the rest of the group was busy making camp so took Zosimos with him.

"Follow me, my friend." Bion cleared the camp and called his protectors and teachers over to him.

"Callus, Petra, come and say hello." Bion used spoken word as well as telepathic communication just so Zosimos could be clear that he had called to them.

"Let me introduce you to Zosimos. Zosimos, this is Callus and Petra." The two tigers bowed and then went to Bion to show their affection. Zosimos was speechless and now Bion spoke to the tigers only.

"Thank you, my friends. How long will you be with us for?"

"Abraxas has asked us to join him in Atlantis. He fears he will have need of us."

"Will you be travelling with us or will you continue to keep your distance?" Bion asked.

"Whatever you would prefer."

"I would be very happy for you to walk with me, for I like your company."

From that moment on, the tigers remained at Bion's side, much to the Lemurians' disbelief.

"Our high priest has been born anew," Zosimos said. "He even seems to be able to talk to these creatures."

***

By the time that they reached Atlantis, they were met by greetings of celebration, which left the Lemurians awestruck. Suddenly the crowd went quiet and all began to kneel at the arrival of Maeja, Abraxas and I.

I walked in the centre, wearing a white dress with edgings of fine gold. Maeja accompanied me to my left, while Abraxas walked on my right. This was a demonstration of beauty, grace, splendour and power. It was a vision that would live in their memories for a long time.

"This is my companion, guardian and friend Maeja." Bion had only seen Maeja in the joining's, but now with her standing in front of him, left him with a certain level of awe at the power she commanded by her presence. Maeja looked at the tigers directly and they bowed then walked behind her and sat down.

"I believe you have already had the pleasure of meeting Abraxas."

"Yes, although I would not say the memory was entirely pleasurable." We both laughed.

I turned towards some priests that had made their way through the crowd, they gestured for Bion to follow them.

With the memories of what his city had turned into still haunting him Zosimos stepped forward rather aggressively and demanded; "Where are you taking our high priest?" Bion held out his arm; at the same time Maeja stood to attention closely followed by the tigers, to which I put my hand on Maeja's back to calm her, this was noticed by both Bion and Zosimos, Maeja relaxed but she did not sit. Bion now turned to Zosimos.

"These people are our friends, our being here is not by chance; we have been invited here, so let's not start off in a manner that is not befitting our training. I am sure that if you ask politely, you will receive a direct and truthful answer."

Zosimos looked humbled but now he stepped forward and explained his sudden rudeness with a better level of politeness.

"My apologies, it's just that where we come from, we have been hunted and persecuted by our temple."

"Yet here you are with more coming; please allow me to apologize, I know of your plight each and every one of you. We are not taking him away; he is the high priest of Lemuria and he will be treated as such. I have learned that he has been in our forests for some time, he is in need of fresh clothes and a hot wash, he has suffered the most and his position needs to be respected, as does mine."

That was as much a gesture of kindness towards the high priest as it was a warning to Zosimos and he understood. As I turned to leave, Maeja did not move or remove her stare from Zosimos until I called out to her.

"Maeja, come stop playing with your food."

Bion tried not to laugh.

"Priestess, that will give him bad dreams," exclaimed Bion quietly.

"No worse than the ones you had after Abraxas finished with you." Now all four of them laughed.

"How did you know of that incident?"

"We have kept watch over you since you set foot on our soil.

***

Earlier that month, Hypatia had called the entire priesthood together, as a new high priest had not been appointed. They had been called to the central chamber for an audience, once all were present, I walked into the centre of the crystal circle. Maeja sat outside the circle looking outwards towards the priests and at Claritia, who was the only priestess present.

Hypatia had prepared me on what would be needed to ensure a smooth transition for Bion. I gently closed my eyes and waited for Hypatia to make her presence felt. I was levitated five feet in the air, my hair shone white and my skin took on a translucent sheen. Being the keepers of records, the priests knew that in the entire time of Atlantis, an event such as this had never been recorded, yet another first and it would not be the last. All the crystals in the entire temple lit up, closely followed by Hypatia, which caused the priests to fall to their knees.

A cloud came out of Hypatia and into me; she then spoke through me.

"Gaia has graciously allowed me to use her as a conduit. I have done this so that there can be no confusion or misunderstanding as to where the authenticity of this instruction has come from or whom the author is. The man who is leading the first of our refugees is the true high priest of Lemuria. He has worked closely with the earth-mother, obeying her laws and honouring her sacredness. Powers higher than I have decreed that he will be the next high priest of Atlantis; so it is said, so shall it be."

The entire room said in unison. "So shall it be."

Bion's insertion into the temple was now assured. After Bion had bathed and changed into some new clothes, he was brought before me.

"Bion, Hypatia has asked that you be brought before her for an audience, you are about to meet a very powerful being. What you will see as a solid object, you should know that she is very much alive and the soul of Atlantis."

"I understand, Gaia."

"Bion, this is the central chamber. No priest is allowed in this chamber without my presence. The only person who may enter is priestess Claritia. If you are in need of Hypatia's advice, then she will speak through me."

Bion didn't say a word and was in awe of the chamber. "Bion, do you have any questions?"

Still Bion said nothing, he was just looking and taking in the splendour of this place that was to be his new home albeit temporary. I asked the question again.

"Sorry, priestess, never before have I seen such splendour, our temple was built on the foundation of the principles of mother-earth. It is plain, moderately furnished and decorated, while this is elaborate and beautiful."

"Hypatia thanks you for your words, she tells me that this was built by the matriarch, who was not of this world, however, it replicates the halls that she knows as home."

***

That night Zosimos was summoned to the temple. A priest came to meet with him from the order of record keepers. "The high priestess has asked for you; will you please follow me."

Zosimos had been witness to what would happen to people who had been summoned by the priest in the night hours, so he had no reason to believe that this situation was any different.

"Why am I being summoned in the late hours?" he

asked. "Could it not wait till daylight hours?"

"All will be explained," was all that the priest said.

That walk was the longest walk that Zosimos had taken. Each step was a step closer to his doom. *What had happened to Bion?* he wondered. *What did she mean by "don't play with your food"?* The questions just kept on and on in his mind.

The walk took them through the gardens and to a side of the temple that was not a usual entrance. At the entrance, Maeja and I were waiting for them. The level of fear shot up and through Zosimos's stomach.

"Thank you that will be all." The priest left the way he came; when it was clear that he was gone, Maeja left also. Zosimos could not contain himself any longer.

"What is the meaning of this? What have you done to my friend?"

"Please allow me to apologise for the manner in which you have been brought here," I said. "I assure you that you are quite safe."

"Well, I am sorry, but your words mean nothing to me," he said nervously.

"Maeja," I called out. Maeja came out from the shadows with Bion at her side, looking better than Zosimos had ever seen him before.

"Oh, Bion," Zosimos said as they hugged each other. "I feared for your safety."

"I have never been in better hands," Bion said. "For these people have planned our rescue with the earth-mother, and I have been in talks with Gaia and Maeja for quite some time. You were chosen too, my friend. It is by no chance that you come to be in Atlantis."

"You have me intrigued, Bion, please explain?"

Clear dialogue had been established, at which point we escorted the men to a secluded part of the garden where they could continue their conversation in private. Bion explained all that Zosimos needed to know, with the exception of Agartha, and by the time he had finished I could feel that Zosimos was awash with questions.

"Zosimos, I feel that you need to rest now, we will revisit this tomorrow with Bion. Maeja will escort you back to where you are dwelling until tomorrow, in the morning you will be brought before the priests so they can finish what we have started here tonight."

The thought of Maeja escorting him made Zosimos nervous, he could still hear in his head, *"Maeja don't play with your food,"* it ran shivers down his spine.

"You know he fears Maeja deeply, Gaia, why do you tease him so."

"Tell me, Bion, did you feel intimidation when you woke up surrounded by the tigers in the forest?"

"I felt more than just intimidation."

"Yet you learned to respect the forest and animals that lived there."

"This is also true." Bion could find no fault in what I was saying.

"Do you not feel that Zosimos has the same ability to learn as you?"

"Well I suppose he does." Bion was being schooled and he knew it.

"Maeja is in full control of who she is, she has a greater understanding of the nature of things than all who serve the temple. If I or Maeja felt that Zosimos had a soul or mind that could turn him in the same way that your mad priest turned, then he would have been dealt with in the forest by my friends."

"The tigers?" Bion said.

"Yes the tigers."

"And they were left with me for that same purpose."

"Yes they were. As for my humour and having fun with Zosimos, ask him tomorrow how his walk went."

Chapter Twenty-One

Friend or Foe

Their walk took them towards the outskirts of the city and Zosimos was sure that this was to be where he was going to meet his end; although he was new to the city, he knew that this was not a direct route to his dwelling. Thoughts of deceit were still at the forefront of his mind as he considered what game I was playing with him.

Maeja had linked in with him and could hear his thoughts, but knew that he was not wise of the ways of Atlantis, so this was an important lesson to learn before he took on the role of head priest.

Maeja stopped and sat in wait until Callas and Petrus appeared with a young buck. Once a week Maeja would leave for the forest in wait for an animal that was to sustain her with nourishment; this had long been the way for her, as the days of her hunting had long since passed.

Callus and Petra stopped just short of Maeja, who remained sat as the buck bowed in front of her. To Zosimos, they were just looking at each other, but to the animals that were present, a prayer was being said and Maeja was honouring the buck's sacrifice. Maeja then stood up and made her way toward the buck, looked at Zosimos, and then put her head to the buck's sweet spot and ended his life. It was clean and quick. The buck's soul was allowed to leave its body just prior to the strike, so as not to feel the fear of death in the afterlife. Maeja then stood back and allowed Callus and Petra to take their fill from the kill, leaving a leg for Maeja. Maeja ate the leg, turned to Zosimos and bowed to him slightly, she then turned to look at the tigers who left towards the temple and she turned towards the town.

Zosimos was still sitting in disbelief as to what he had just witnessed when he realized that Maeja had stopped and was now looking at him, he soon realized that he was to follow. He clumsily rose to his feet and quickly but not too gracefully joined her and they were on their way to his dwelling.

Zosimos felt belittled by the whole experience, but honoured to witness such a sacred moment. He was beginning to see that he had no need to fear Maeja and she could see that he was settling down, which pleased her.

Having returned to his dwelling, Zosimos thanked her for allowing him to watch the sacrifice that had taken place, he then did something that he was to soon curse himself for, he stretched out his hand to pet her at which she let out a roar. Zosimos saw the ferocity in her eyes it was unmistakable; instantly he dropped to his knees, lowered his head, closed his eyes and asked for her forgiveness, and when he opened his eyes all he saw was her vanishing into the night.

"Is all well, Maeja?" I asked her when she entered my chamber.

"Yes, Gaia, he understands now; he will be fine."

Maeja was sitting next to me as I stroked her head and paying particular attention to her ears as this filled Maeja with much pleasure. To look at her in this vulnerable position you could quite easily make the mistake of thinking that she was as tame as a rabbit, a fact that would occasionally bring a smile to my face.

"Did you really need to show him that he was not as close to you as he thought?"

"You would have done the same, we both know that if we have the opportunity to have fun, we will take it."

"You two will get me into trouble." Hypatia had joined into the conversation. She often would as our bond and friendship was a blessed one.

"Oh, Hypatia," I said. "You enjoyed it as much as we did."

"Actually, yes I did, it will be a shame that it will have to end, but end it will."

"Hypatia, will we still be together when that day

comes?" I asked.

"No, child, but we will be part of a bigger family and our roles will be different to the ones that we have here."

"How so?"

"I will show you in a vision while you sleep, in the near future."

"You tease." I was not too pleased at the prospect of having to wait for a glimpse of what I could expect.

Maeja laughed. "Oh the high priestess doesn't like to be played with, what a surprise." Now we were all laughing, which woke Claritia, whose chamber joined onto mine.

"Oh, Claritia, we apologise," I said. "Come join us. It has been a busy day."

I spoke openly and relayed back what Maeja and Hypatia were saying, by now Claritia was part of the inner circle but not connected. I did my best to relay all that was being said, which was quite difficult because of the level of fun and the quickness of the responses. Hypatia was clearly getting frustrated with the flow of fun that we were all having. "Oh this is ridiculous, Claritia, hear me now." The look on Claritia's face was a picture and most definitely fitted in with the mood. Claritia now had full ability to hear both Hypatia and Maeja. Hypatia had opened up her ability to telecommunicate. Now the tempo rose and continued for the remainder of the night. Before we realized it, Abraxas entered my chamber. "Oh, I see you are up and excited about our journey," he said. "Hypatia must have told you." At the sound of 'journey', Maeja and I looked at Abraxas in surprise, who in turn was in a place of embarrassment.

"Oh dear, she has not told you?" he enquired.

"Hypatia, is there something you wish to share at this point?" I said.

"Oops, well you can only blame yourselves," she said. "We were having so much fun." This was true, however Abraxas was beginning to get a clearer picture of what was transpiring.

"Hypatia, you have kept them up and you know what we have to do?"

"Abraxas, calm down. I have kept her energy up and clear... she will be fine."

"Oh, really," Abraxas said. "That would explain why she now sleeps?"

"I am fine Abraxas; I am just resting my eyes."

"We will see." He was clearly agitated and in no mood for fun. The short trip to Agartha had him worried and he had wished to return.

Hypatia suggested that he took me with him as she put it, "It would be good for all concerned."

"Gaia, get yourself ready we are going to Agartha, I have business there and we have yet to return what is theirs."

I did not need telling twice, in no time at all I was looking excited and ready to go. Maeja was sent to retrieve Zosimos from his dwelling. Zosimos was ready and eager to see what the day was to bring, the thought of him being in service again filled him with much joy. Maeja took the lead followed by Zosimos, he was not about to make the same mistake again. He did not notice Callus and Petra joining them from behind and when he did the first thing he saw was the tigers licking their lips and whiskers, Maeja had also noticed.

"Leave him be, he has had quite enough of our humour."

"You take our fun, I so much like to smell his fear it amuses us." Petra the female had a young mind and clearly was not ready for the serious life of the temple but that would have to change.

"Yes me too but this must stay a serious matter, it is temple business." Maeja's reply was sharp as this was set to be the beginning of Zosimos's initiation into the brotherhood of record keepers. It was to be my final instruction before I left for Agartha.

We all met at the entrance to the temple of record keepers, when the formalities were dealt with I informed him that he was to be taken into the temple, where he would receive instruction as to his duties and responsibilities, at which point four priests came through the door to receive him. "These priests will take you to your chambers and prepare you, from this moment on I hand over my responsibility of you to the brotherhood, you will no longer have any dealings with me, my only contact to you will be through the high priest." With that I mounted Abraxas and we were gone.

"I see you have the responsibility of holding the weight of the heart stone this time, my friend." I could feel the energy of the heart stone, I took more notice of it now and if I had not witnessed it myself, I would not have known that the power of this crystal was possibly as strong as Hypatia.

"Yes, Gaia; for I feared with your lack of proper rest that the weight of this gem would have been too much for your delicate arms to hold."

It was true for I was feeling the pinch in my eyes but I would have time to rest, I was sure of it.

Chapter Twenty-Two

A Blessed Time

The journey to Agartha was a pleasurable affair. I took the time to look at Atlantis from my heightened viewpoint, which was a fantastic experience. I had astral travelled in the times when Maeja, Hypatia and I had travelled to Lemuria to join with Ianthe and the others. However, to be physically on the back of Abraxas and flying through the skies, was a feeling that astral projection could not come close to. At times, I would put my hands out, making it feel like I was flying and not Abraxas. He filled me with great wonderment as he soared so high. At times I had trouble finding my breath and I felt like a child again, so much so that I linked in with Maeja.

"Oh, Maeja, this is unbelievable. I wish you were here."

"I am, or I should say we are; Hypatia and I are watching you, but to be honest, animals such as I am, are not meant to be where the birds live, as it violates the natural laws that I live by."

"Your loss wheeee…" I exclaimed. Abraxas had just done a loop and twist.

Maeja was not too impressed.

"Oh, Maeja, lighten up. This is my treat and I am enjoying it, so let me be."

On our arrival, Ianthe and Timo were already waiting for us. Their powers and sense of feeling had grown tremendously and on reflection, it was clear that they had well established themselves into this new society.

It had not been too long since I had last visited Agartha, and to my surprise, the transformation was a massive achievement. Even Abraxas was suitably impressed.

"Hello to you all, I have brought Gaia, who is looking forward to spending some time with her friends. This will be my last visit here, and my purpose is to establish what kind of energy shrouds this place, and to ascertain how your integration in this sacred space is forming. But before we continue I wish to apologise for my rudeness on my last visit." It was clear that everybody without exception understood.

"Timo, I feel that you are the key to this energy, as it feels crystalline in its nature. Can you explain what this is, as it has concerned me since my last visit and I have concerns into how you intend to develop the city?"

"Abraxas, when Ourania was taken, my crystals informed me that a dangerous energy had inserted itself onto the power grid of Demeta. On hearing Petrus's description of the elders, we knew that they had delved into Demeta's structure. As a result, on instructions from Demeta, we put up defences to protect this location."

I was now very intrigued: "You can do this, Timo?"

"Yes, Gaia. I have learnt so much in my time here and have made some extremely powerful friends."

"Please explain," Abraxas said curiously.

"Kallias has shown me a chamber that the earth-mother guided him to," Timo said. "He has developed quite a skill for the energy patterns of the crystals. We were taken to a place where she has been developing crystals in readiness for our arrival. She knew that with the help of the crystals we would achieve so much. Some of the crystals that she has asked us to gather form a protective barrier in Agartha, while some of the crystals are helping us to build and construct our homes."

Abraxas was happy with what he was hearing and knew that Agartha would be safe from the decay of the civilisations that would take over on the surface of the planet. He wanted to talk to Ianthe and Silas, which gave me the opportunity to talk with Timo.

"Timo," I said. "How have you found things here? Are the people settling down well?"

"Truthfully, priestess, it is all that we had hoped for. Demeta has done all that was promised... and more. The earth here is so rich that anything that is planted grows. She has shown me so much with the crystals that I feel I know more than Hypatia. Please don't tell her I said that!" We both laughed.

"So, tell me about Kallias, is he more than just a talented person who has grasped the crystals?"

Timo blushed, "How could you tell?"

"Your energy fluttered every time you called his name."

"Oh, please forgive me, priestess."

"Timo, we both knew that you were to have a companion, not to mention to bring little ones into the world, so what are you not telling me."

I was showing my playful side; the time for business had now passed.

"He is such a caring man, he is passionate, strong and he listens, even when I am not talking. It is as if we are truly one. If I am thinking about a project, he will offer solutions, even before I tell him there is a problem. Together, we have managed to construct a hall of wisdom. This hall is where we store our crystals. We are in the middle of constructing a power centre for the crystals; when that is complete, we will move all the crystals there."

"That sounds marvellous; may I visit it?"

"I was hoping you would say that," she said, her voice was full of excitement. "It is my pet project."

As we walked to the power centre, Timo explained further.

"The power that these crystals harness is incredible; we just need to understand them for their full potential to be realised. Kallias has been of great help in this matter, his perception in reading energy has been a great benefit to me in so many areas. The power that the crystals possess is helping us to construct what we need much quicker. We have learnt how to format energy to make a force that helps to penetrate the crystals. This energy is destructive in its natural form but we have learnt how to harness this energy and direct it to where we need it to go. We then developed the ability to raise or lower the amount of energy that is released, making it a more reliable and stable element to work with. Once this was achieved, working with the crystals took on a completely different meaning. The people of Agartha have benefited by this immensely; all the people that are here are working towards a common goal, which is the completion of a civilisation that rivals Atlantis and Lemuria using knowledge from both cultures to build a new one."

As Timo continued, I did not have to use any latent gifts to see and feel the level of excitement that she was expressing, it was truly beautiful to see.

"The power centre will hold all the crystals; we will establish a workforce, who we believe to have the correct attitude and energy to work with the crystals. Ionas and Miltiades are working on instrumentations to help with the reading and storing of power and the care of the crystals. When it is complete, we will link the centre with the city so that all will be able to utilise this new and exciting energy."

They had arrived at the centre and Kallias was directing people as to where to place a curious object. "What is happening here?" I asked. "By the way, Kallias looks so much better in the flesh… you have picked well, Timo."

"You are terrible, priestess." Timo was blushing again.

"Wait a minute," I said. "It's not just an infatuation is it? You two have joined."

Now Timo was blushing furiously.

"Timo, calm yourself." I was overjoyed at the news, however, my laughter made Timo's embarrassment even worse.

Timo composed herself and continued: "Priestess, stop, lest you make me lose the respect of the people."

"I don't think you are going to need my help for that."

"Priestess!"

"Oh, let me have my fun," I said. "Atlantis has become so serious."

"The object," Timo said.

"OK, business it is then."

Kallias came over to join us. "I am happy to see you again, priestess, I must tell you it brings me great pleasure to be able to actually talk to you."

"It is also a pleasure to hear your voice," I said. "It brings me joy to know that Abraxas was able to restore your power of the spoken word, which I see has served you well."

Timo kicked me.

"Please excuse her, Kallias, it seems that the journey here has affected her ability to think clearly."

Kallias had a slight flush in his cheeks as he replied: "Thank you, priestess. Timo, we are ready for you." He tried to hide his embarrassment and I smiled as to say that it did not work.

The people who were with Kallias had moved to a spot that was designated to be a safe area to stand and wait for Timo. Timo walked over to an object; it was a golden case which I could see was holding a crystal. Attached to the case was a metallic-looking rope. Timo picked up a gold plate with a crystal housed in its centre, which she placed over her chest. She stood in front of the device, in her hand was a small box that had a dial of sorts. Timo blessed the crystal and asked the earth-mother for guidance. "Make it strong; make it true."

"Make what strong and true?" I was impatient to understand.

"Wait," Kallias instructed. "You will see."

Timo turned the dial and the rope directed light towards the device, which shot a beam of light into her chest. Suddenly, the ground shook and a pillar began to rise out of the earth. It rose fifty feet and then stopped... then a second and a third. This continued until twelve pillars were standing tall and proud. I watched on with shock and awe at what was happening here, not feeling able to speak until the last pillar was raised. I rushed over to where Timo had gone down to her knees.

"What in the goddess's name has just happened here?"

I asked. Timo was fine but weak, and she was thanking mother-earth for her strength.

"Timo, what have I just witnessed?" I asked.

"A moment please, priestess," Kallias said, "Timo needs water." One of the helpers was already giving Timo some water, and then slowly she got back on her feet.

"Priestess," Timo said. "I work with the crystals and mother-earth to make what buildings we need, this centre is of mother's design, she suggested that we construct this and this is the way of it. Because of my connection to the crystals I am a part of them as they are to me. Demeta understands this on levels that I am just beginning to understand as such we work together and share the work, the crystals love and protect me so I am never in danger. She knows it drains me but I insist on the amount that gets done, she is a loving provider who will not allow me to over extend my energy. When we complete a piece of work she replaces what energy that I use, it is a symbiotic relationship."

"I never thought for a moment that you had become such a person... you have certainly grown," I said. "These people are blessed to have you; I am also blessed to have witnessed what you have become. Tell me, Timo, how does this work?"

"Demeta gives me the permission that I need to create from her soil what is needed. The pillars that were erected came directly from Demeta's body. The crystal gave us the connection that was needed to bring the whole process together, which is a co-operation of soul, body and mind. Demeta provides the material and the vision, whereby the crystals provide the correct level of energy to activate the soil. I provide the will and desire to construct."

"Could Demeta not do this on her own?" I asked.

"She probably could but she wanted me to be a part of this process. She knew that the people of Agartha would have more respect for the work carried out if they had an understanding of the process."

I could see that Timo had given this a lot of thought;

the whole situation actually made sense, we continued our discussion as Timo took me around the remaining parts of the growing city.

***

Abraxas was in deep discussion with Silas about the animals and how the Lemurians were handling the way that the Atlanteans interacted with them.

"The Lemurians have a relationship with the earth that is not fully understood by the Atlanteans, so the balance is perfect," Silas explained. "They complement each other; it is a perfect blending of cultures, in time they will both understand their roles in this society. Presently, the Lemurians are administering to the needs for nourishment, whereas the Atlanteans are administering the needs for shelter and power."

"Is there no sharing of knowledge?" Abraxas asked curiously.

"We have established a hall for the blending of knowledge, this was one of our first constructions when we had full knowledge of the power that Timo and Kallias had discovered. We share the knowledge of the two cultures through our children, which we call the temple of new life, the priestesses and priests from Atlantis and Lemuria are administering to this process, and in time, Chrysanta will train even more."

Abraxas turned his attention to Ianthe. "And what about you, Ianthe?"

"At present, I am spending my time in the fields that we have planted with the Lemurians. Petrus has been teaching me so much and we brought many herbs and roots. It has kept me busy, but more importantly, I felt the need to form a stronger bond with the earth-mother. I have come to understand that the reason why I was sent to Lemuria was to integrate with her and learn what I could about healing. I work a lot with my father, and I am helping the people and the animals equally. With Petrus's help, I have expanded my mental abilities and I am able to communicate with mother directly. Actually, it has been quite a magical journey for all of us."

Abraxas was extremely happy with what he saw and felt. However, it was now time to go. And while there were no goodbyes, that would be the last time that they would see Abraxas in Agartha. We left Agartha in the same manner that we came, however I was now feeling a tinge of longing in my soul, I knew that Abraxas could feel this but he left me to my thoughts until I eventually spoke.

"Abraxas, let's not go directly home. I wish to see the land."

Abraxas was happy to oblige and he flew around the coast, over mountains, through valleys, and then showed me the place he once called home. We talked at great length, until the time had come for us to return home.

Chapter Twenty-Three

The Passing

On our arrival in Atlantis, Maeja was walking the halls accompanied by Claritia. While little was said as to how long we would be gone, Maeja didn't think that we would have returned so soon.

"Was there a problem in Agartha that brings you back so quickly?" she asked.

"Why no, Maeja," I said. "We did what we had to."

Abraxas was on his way to M's chamber to spend time with Hypatia. I knew that Maeja would be walking the halls with Claritia, and when I found them, Claritia went to her chamber and left us to talk. The pair of us were in no mood to retire, so we walked and talked well into the night.

The following day, Hypatia summoned us to her chamber: "Gaia and Maeja, come to me."

On entering the chamber, Abraxas was waiting for us and holding a serious energy pattern.

"OK, what have we done now?" I asked, trying to lighten the mood but to no avail.

"It is time to put your business in order," Hypatia said.

"We are leaving!" Maeja stated with a certain level of assertiveness.

"Yes, Maeja; we will wait until you have put things in order, but we will not wait for long."

We all knew that this moment would come; still, there was an element of sorrow and finality attached to leaving a city so full of friends. I thought about Ourania, the strength of will she had shown to leave Atlantis, knowing that she was heading to a place that would mark the end of her journey on this plane. I believed that this was a private thought, but I was to receive a surprise.

"Gaia, you are heading to a place where you will have

so much to do, along with so many friends."

I nearly wept right there and then. "Ourania!" I cried out. This was an unexpected surprise. "Oh, Ourania, I have missed you so much. To hear your voice brings me so much joy. Oh, Ourania, will we meet again? Hearing your voice gives me the courage to do what has to be done. How is it that you come to be here?"

"I have always been here, my child, watching over you." Maeja could feel the emotion building up in me and moved closer to give me some support, for she knew what was coming. I didn't even notice just how tightly I was holding on to Maeja's fur as the tears came streaming out of me.

"Oh, my sweet child, don't upset yourself so," Ourania said. "Yes, we will meet again, but for now you have work to do. I leave you with Hypatia until we meet in the hereafter." She was gone as quickly as she came.

"Maeja," I said. "I heard her voice and felt her energy... it really was her, and she still calls me sweet child."

Yes, if only she knew the truth, Maeja thought.

"Maeja!" I yelled at her and gave her a slap on the back of her head. We laughed.

"Gaia, do what you need to do," Hypatia said. "I leave it all in your hands. Maeja, tell Callus and Petra to fully integrate themselves to Bion and Zosimos, for they will need protecting in the years to come. Teach them what it means to be guardians to the temple. I will assist you if you are in need. We leave twenty days from this point. Goddess speed to you both."

Maeja looked at me with a sense of pride and excitement, but what she got back in return was a look of fear and anticipation, for I was not ready. I didn't know how this transition was going to happen.

We left the chamber and Abraxas went to the forest to find an old friend, who was as old as the earth itself. He was known as the emperor crystal; who had been guarded in a cave by animals, and by Demeta. On this planet he

had no name, however, he carried the blueprint for earth.
"Hallo, my old friend," Abraxas said. "How have the years
been for you?"

"Abraxas, well, well, well. The years have been good
but they could have been better if my friends would visit
more often. I knew you had not departed yet as I could feel
your essence and Demeta keeps me informed. So, what
brings a welcomed stranger to my lonely hollow?"

"You always had a flair for drama," Abraxas said. "My
time has come, my friend. I depart on summer's eve."

"Then it is business that brings you to me."

"Yes it is. As you may well know, the plan for Agartha
is now a reality. Demeta has kept you well informed, so
you will know that I hold the key to her gate."

The key to the gate of Demeta was a mystical key,
which concealed the entrance from prying eyes, leaving
only a skilled practitioner of mystical arts to find it.

"It is now my sworn duty to pass on the key," Abraxas
said. "I know of no other animal, person or entity that is
more fitting for this task… an entity that has stood the test
of time and has no agenda other than the protection of this
planet. Will you accept this responsibility, my friend?"

"I will be honoured to be the keeper of the key."

Abraxas then touched the emperor crystal with his
horn. At the point of contact, there was an explosion of
energy of such force, that it knocked Abraxas to his knees
and sent a shockwave throughout the lands of all
kingdoms. There was not a soul who could escape the
sensation, as it penetrated the cells of every living thing.

"Ianthe, did you feel that?" Timo felt it the most due to
her link to the crystals.

"Yes, Timo, and by the looks of things, everybody else
felt it too. What was it and what does it mean?"

"It feels as though a very powerful ancient soul has
been awakened. I picked up an energy that was very old,"
Timo said. "That's all I know."

"Hypatia, what was that?" I asked. It has made me and
Maeja feel quite ill in our stomachs?"

In Lemuria, the mad priest had felt it too; however, he had no idea that it was to mark the end of Lemuria. He was so shaken that he had no other thought but to flee. The people were now beginning to challenge his rule over them and they were attacking the guards with hit-and-run tactics. He went to his stockpile of acquired gold and trinkets and began to load them onto a boat in a secret subway river, but as he was doing so, all the stonework and walls around him began to crumble.

The activation of the emperor prompted earth-mother to start the cleansing. It triggered her to open up a subterranean plate that caused a major earthquake. This triggered a tidal wave that would engulf Lemuria, thus wiping it off the face of the earth.

All that was planned had accumulated to this moment, the mad priest had made it out to open water and felt safe now that he could see the ship that he was to take to distant shores, once there he would be rich and want for nothing. In the distance he could see something on the horizon. At first it looked like a large wave, nothing too serious but he soon realized that this was no normal wave; he could feel the power of it as his little boat began to speed up towards it, he could not begin to imagine what was happening but he soon would. He looked at the ship and in the time that it took him to see Lemuria and look back at the ship the wave had grown tenfold, he then realized that all was lost.

"Gaia, did you feel Demeta flex?"

"Yes I did, Maeja." At that moment, Demeta and Hypatia addressed all who had knowledge of the coming event. Demeta addressed the Agarthans leaving Hypatia to address Maeja, Abraxas and I.

"We have started the cleansing and from here on there will be no more Lemuria." Although all knew what was coming, the finality of the statement felt so chilling. The whole event took less than ten minutes to complete. I could feel every soul whose light was extinguished in the cleansing, and I wept for each of those souls.

Demeta spoke to me directly: "Gaia, why do you weep

so? We all knew this had to happen."

"Yes, but those poor souls," I said.

"Those poor souls as you put it were masters of their own fate. You are well aware, that the people who lived as was intended were spared, and have settled in places that would sustain them. The souls that are left in Lemuria will reincarnate to work out their wrongful deeds on this planet in later lives. This is the way the creator intended the soul to live, despite a select few having volunteered to reincarnate as dauphins. This is an agreement that was made by those souls before they incarnated on this world in this time. All this knowledge you know and understand. Gaia, I am not telling you something you do not know."

"Yes, I do know this, Demeta, but I still feel their pain. Am I wrong to have empathy for these poor souls?"

"No you are not," Demeta said. "But you cannot carry their pain and suffering. You must learn to detach yourself from it, for where you are going you will witness much and see things that you may wish to intercede. Only the creator can give dispensation to a living being. Do you understand what I am telling you?"

"I hear you, Demeta, but please allow me to mourn over those that are lost."

"As you wish, Gaia... as you wish."

Bion was in his chamber. He had just attended the ceremony for high priest when the energy wave hit him. Petra decided that she wanted to stay with Bion, and she too had felt the sickening feeling of Lemuria being cleansed. The pair had felt each other's emotions, the feeling of the loss being particularly heavy for Bion.

That night I saw my departure in a vision. I woke in the morning and Maeja could see a marked improvement in me. Maeja did not fear much, but she sensed that I was having difficulty accepting our final destination.

"You look better today, princess." Maeja had not called me that since I was a child.

"Yes, my little fluff ball, I feel like I can take on the world."

In the days that followed Maeja was having trouble keeping up with me. It had not been long since a new head priestess was appointed. The ceremony took place alongside Bion's ceremony, I knew that I would be the last high priestess and that these two people would be sharing the responsibility of Atlantis which would help with the integration of the Lemurian people into Atlantean society. A typical day would pass with me overseeing six birthing ceremonies; twelve naming ceremonies for Lemurians who wanted Atlantean names, two passing-over ceremonies, these I did not enjoy. It was always taught that the soul moves on easiest in the dark hours, so the passing-over ceremonies was done at high night. Now that all was done for this day I could relax. Days like this were many as I wanted to ensure that I left Atlantis in good hands; with each passing day I stepped back just a little to allow the new leadership to insert themselves into the hearts of the Atlantean people.

The morning finally arrived that marked the end of the twenty-day period. I was feeling a little apprehensive about today but mildly excited. Maeja had done her morning inspection, as the priestesses liked to call it and was back in my chambers.

"Are you ready, Gaia?"

"Yes, I believe I am."

We left for M's chamber and on our arrival, Abraxas was there waiting.

"Ah, all are present even the reluctant child." Abraxas, in the days after we went to Agartha, did like to tease me. I had a smile on my face. Abraxas had become more at ease at the prospect of leaving this long-extended stay on the planet.

"This reluctant child can't wait to see the looks on everyone's faces when we depart."

"Well, enough said... let us prepare." With that,

Hypatia raised her harmonic tone, which signalled all crystals throughout Atlantis and Agartha to raise theirs. Timo, Ianthe, Chrysanta and Silas were sent for and had arrived during the night; however, their arrival was kept from Maeja and I. At the sounding of the harmonic tone, all those who served the temple knew that they had to gather at the central chamber.

When all were present (including the animals), Timo and Ianthe led the precession of priestesses and priests outside to a central courtyard, the same place that the people had gathered to witness the birth of their new high priestess – me. The priestesses and priests were stood in the front and the crowd gathered behind them. When Hypatia could see that all were present, she lowered the wall that kept this chamber a secret. "This will not be needed anymore but it does need a little refresher." No sooner did she say that, when a portrait of Maeja, Abraxas and I appeared on the wall.

"I think you have over-exaggerated Maeja's splendour," I said, at which I received a slap from Maeja.

"I owed you that, and stop complaining you big baby." Abraxas and Hypatia were quietly laughing. Maeja and Abraxas led the way to the balcony; when the crowd were silent, I appeared making my presence felt and I addressed the sea of people.

"I, Gaia, high priestess of Atlantis, have been given a great charge for which I will be ever grateful."

It was now at this point when I saw my dearest friend with her sister and father who threw me off guard and I lost my words. Timo who was well known by the Atlanteans came up onto the balcony.

"The high priestess loves you all dearly." Timo was now looking directly into my eyes whilst petting Maeja's ears whilst she said what she felt was needed to be said.

"The powers-that-be have decided that it is time for a new era in Atlantis; with the arrival of our cousins from Lemuria, things must and will change. The ways of the high priestess and great crystal has come to an end and the responsibility is now being passed on to the high priest and head priestess." I had recomposed myself, gathered my thoughts and gave Timo the biggest hug, for in my mind nobody, not even a friend was going to steal my moment, I was now ready to continue.

"We have consulted with all powers that help to govern these lands and beyond; permission has been given for our ascension. Now witness the power of the great crystal."

I was elated as my friend had come to say goodbye and had given me the strength to finish this. Now, what many people of Atlantis had no idea of, including me, was that Hypatia had the power to transport the crystal to wherever she wished, and whilst I was giving my speech with the help of Timo, Hypatia was making her way to the balcony. Abraxas knew exactly what was going to happen, as he had seen it many times before on other worlds. Knowing that Hypatia was directly behind them, he moved to the side to reveal her. She had never been seen outside of the temple, and the priestesses and priests all knelt and bowed their heads, which signalled for the people to do the same. Hypatia took centre stage and prepared herself to make a speech. This being her last act on the planet, she with the assistance from unseen forces allowed for her speech to be heard physically.

"Rise, my children, I am the great crystal of the temple of light. I am eternal and have stood as guardian over Atlantis since the beginning of her time. You have been good, loyal people to the ways that were given to you by my masters and during that time, I have watched over each and every one of you. People of Lemuria, your society is no more. The people of that land that were left behind, were judged by the almighty and the city had to be cleansed. This was done as an example of what can happen if people fall to the desires of power and greed over love and unity. Learn from what has happened to your homeland and teach future generations as well as your hosts about the perils of the misuse of power. You now have a responsibility to live as the creator intended you to live. Live well and never forget your lost brothers and sisters. Now bear witness to my power!"

Hypatia shone so brightly that the crystal shattered into two pieces which fell to the floor. She took on incorporeal form, then levitated; at the same moment Abraxas, Maeja and I, all rose ten feet from the ground. We all shone as bright as the morning sun on a clear day, so bright that for a moment, everyone looking on was blinded. By the time their vision had returned, the quartet was no more.

Timo, Ianthe, Chrysanta and Silas knew that as soon as the ascension happened that it was time to leave. Questions would be asked, to which the answers would lead people to start to look for Agartha. Trexus had asked three of his brothers to aid him in getting the three of them from Agartha to Atlantis and back. The whole group were in awe at what they just witnessed. They were shielded from the light and what they saw was Maeja, Abraxas and myself, slowly transform into pure energy. Then, one at a time, our energy shot up to the skies in a beam of bright white light, followed by Hypatia. On my ascension, I went to Timo before ascending, kissed her cheek and said, "Thank you. I will be in your dreams."

Timo was moved to tears and she felt a boost of energy, a gift from me that she would later come to understand and use.

Chapter Twenty-Four

What Will Become of Us?

Three weeks had passed since the ascension and Bion still could not stop thinking about the whole affair. The fact that he no longer had me to lean on for advice was difficult for him to deal with. He felt that people needed to believe in him, but more significantly, he needed to believe in himself.

Bion was walking through the halls with Petra, as Maeja had instructed her to remain by his side. Maeja had insisted that they walk the halls first thing every morning, which would give him a good starting point for the day. On this particular day, he found himself in front of the circle of pillars in the central chamber. It looked bare without Hypatia in its centre, and although he had only seen her there once, he could remember it clearly.

"Bion, get out of this melancholy. You have work to do. The people are getting restless and the temple is becoming less than it was, so snap out of it." Bion's first reaction was deep shock then the realization of the identity hit him, he recognised the voice and the energy.

"Ourania?" he questioned himself. *"Am I dreaming or am I going mad? What is this?"*

"No, you are not losing your mind, my friend; however, you are out of your mind if you think that you can have the position of high priest and sit on the reputation of past leaders, and not expect the people to rise up, or expect more from you." Ourania was clearly unhappy with her friend.

"I was high priestess," Ourania continued. "I will not sit by and let you take my good name and the work that has been done in Atlantis go to ruin before its time."

"What would you have me do? The spectacle that Hypatia and the others put on has done me no favours."

"That is your perception not ours."

"Ours?" he enquired. "Who else is with you?"

"That is not for you to know, so do you want my help or not?"

"Oh, it's help you're offering... all this time I thought you had only come to mock me."

"Ah, humour," she said. "Now we are getting somewhere."

"By the look on Petra's face, I am assuming she is getting talked to as well."

"Believe me, Bion, what I have said to you is nothing compared to what Maeja is saying to Petra. I actually feel for her, so, what about it? Do you wish for my guidance?"

"That would be very beneficial to me, Ourania, I do miss your company."

"Careful, my friend. I would not be impressed if the command decided to send me back to keep you company." They both laughed and from that moment on, Bion grew from strength to strength. The ironic truth about the whole affair, is that he didn't really need Ourania's help, just knowing that she was close by gave him the strength and comfort he needed.

***

Atlantis was changing and not for the better. The departure of the high priestess didn't have the desired effect that Bion and the other priests and priestesses had hoped for. It had started with a concern that there would be no high priestess, which was a situation that was unheard of until that day. Furthermore, a stranger to Atlantean ways was sharing the power and authority of Atlantis with the head priestesses, and they had lost the great crystal. The presence of refugees had doubled the population of Atlantis, even after the migration of the Atlanteans to Agartha, Demeta had her eye on the situation but was informed by the galactic command not to interfere as this is what was foreseen and it had to come to pass. The people had to learn to survive and adapt, or be consumed in their own stupidity. Demeta knew the consequences of what was being asked of her, the die was cast and Atlantis was heading the same way as Lemuria.

With the great crystal now gone, some of the priests knew of the dissention in Atlantis, and they felt that with the success that Timo had with crystals that it would be prudent to try to emulate her success. In order for this to succeed, they formed a group for the study and development of crystals. They did this for the betterment of Atlantis, as they felt that the people needed the continuity that was now missing in Hypatia. Bion was reluctant to allow this, but the head priestess advised him that this could be beneficial and needed. Therefore, with the backing of both the head priestess and priest, the order of the central sun was now in service.

The selection process was long and detailed. The agreement was made that there should be an equal number of men and women and that they had to have all the redeeming qualities of purity and dedication for the betterment of Atlantis. If it were felt that a person had an agenda, which was deemed to be for the betterment of one's self, then that person would be removed from the order. After the ascension there were not many people who had experience working with crystals; or the understanding of them, while Bion had had contact with Hypatia, his knowledge of the inner workings of how she and I communicated was a mystery, not only to him, but also to all who now served in the temple. It also transpired that the only people who knew and had helped Timo with the crystals were Hypatia, Maeja, Chrysanta and myself. There was one other who worked closely with Hypatia but she had taken a vow of silence on the day of ascension. Bion tried to contact Demeta regarding the problem but she seemed reluctant to help. Frustration was getting the better of Bion. He badly wanted Atlantis to be a success and not fall into the abyss in the same way that Lemuria had done. He knew he had to do something and hoped that

Demeta had not totally turned her back on him, he knew that he would have to go into a deep meditation.

Bion prepared himself for the whole day; he drank plenty of spring water, ate fruit, nuts and berries, he took all the correct herbs to ensure a deep meditative state. He knew that Demeta would have been watching him, and she would have known that with the herbs that he had ingested, he was serious and wanted answers. When he knew that his body was in the desired state for meditation, he made himself comfortable. He was now ready to find Demeta. "Demeta," he said. "I know you can hear me. We need to talk."

"Bion, I am here… ask what you will."

There was something about her tone that unsettled him.

"Have I wronged you in some way?" he asked.

"Bion, you tamper with things that you do not understand."

"Then help me to understand, for what we do, we do to help Atlantis."

"What was done in Lemuria was done to help Lemuria, and where is it now?"

"Are you telling me that you do not trust our intentions?"

"Your intentions are true, that much I can see. However, it is the free will of the human condition that is in question; not the actions of a minor group of well-intending people, who always start out with the purest of intentions. Those intentions then get manipulated into something entirely different to what they started off as."

"Demeta, please help me to understand why you are so reluctant to help me?"

"Bion, my hands are tied. I cannot help you."

"You cannot or will not?" he asked.

"She cannot, Demeta speaks the truth and you should be ashamed to pressure her so." It was Ourania, who had been linked into their conversation from the beginning.

"Ourania, thank the goddess," Bion said.

"Do not thank me, for I have not come to help you. I

have come to put you back into your rightful place."

"I need help with my people," Bion said. "I don't need to be scolded."

"What you need, Bion, is to remember your place, Bion high priest of Atlantis. Now I suggest that you quieten your mind and let a person who knows of these things show you the error of your ways." Now Bion was angered as well as ashamed to have made a dear friend feel the need to put him down a notch or two.

"You know me, do you not?" It was Hypatia and she sounded unhappy.

"Yes, I do," Bion said. "It seems that I have got a lot of attention."

"Do not presume that this is a good thing Bion, for I am here to tell you that it is not. You have placed a dear friend in a very difficult position. She has tried to help you as much as we will allow her to; at times, she has gone beyond her agreement to her responsibility towards you. As a result, you will now have to deal with me. I will not tolerate your current position on this matter, for it is not for you or any Atlantean to delve into matters concerning crystals. We of the command see all and I tell you this, Bion, crystals will destroy Atlantis after you have passed over. Nevertheless, if you continue to persist in this manner, you will bring about the destruction of more than Atlantis, and that is not for this world. Bion, Demeta has been told by the galactic command, not to interfere; however, she is finding it hard not to. I am now telling you to remember that your time in Atlantis as high priest was never going to be a long tenancy, that much you have forgotten. Your time will soon end, so let the story of Atlantis unfold and stop pushing to try to solve the unsolvable. If you have any questions, direct them to me and I will tell you what you need to know, and no more."

"Have I over-reached?" Bion asked.

"No, not at all, you have acted as the high priest of a once great civilisation, but now you must act like a high priest of a civilisation that is not going to succeed."

"Are you telling me to give up on Atlantis?" he asked.

"No, I am telling you to be wiser than those around you. I am telling you it is time to wake up and stop blaming the ascension for your smites. You have everything you need to help these people but what you fail to see is that they do not want your help. They want to do it for themselves and they will fail, for they do not have the support of the command."

"And what of me?"

"Your path and destiny is unchanged, stay on the path."

By the time Bion had come back to reality, he knew that he had come close to losing his way. He would have to take greater care as well as being mindful of his thoughts; as in his own private moments, he believed that they had failed him. He would have to learn how to detach himself from this situation, but he wondered. *"How can I find the strength to look people in the eye and tell them that all was well?"*

"We will help you." Bion was not aware that the link was still active. "Yes, the link will always be active. We just choose to remain quiet, to give you the chance to be."

"Again, really?" Yet another thought that had slipped.

"Still active."

"Sweet, goddess. I can't even think on my own."

"Still here."

"OK, OK, I get the message." Be it conscious thought, subconscious thought or verbal communication, he would have company to help keep him on the correct path.

***

There was talk in Atlantis of a man who was said to have studied under the old high priest. It was said that the old high priest had knowledge of growing and developing crystals. If this priest had such knowledge, the question posed, was whether he shared that knowledge. It was said that the man was once a priest at the temple he was close to the ex-high priest but left the temple suddenly, no clear reason was ever given or explained. The priest's name was Macedon.

Macedon had left for the outskirts of Atlantis away from prying eyes to study further, he was aware what Kaius was doing and he felt that he could continue with the work that was done. He had made some significant progress with the crystals that Kaius had formed, but needed more. Kaius had collected and grown some quite powerful crystals, which Macedon had managed to find and work with. Still, he knew that for his progression to bear fruit, he would have to develop a more powerful crystal, so he devoted his work to this sole purpose.

There was also a man who took a great interest in the development of the temple. Kallicticus would not rest until he saw the downfall of the temple. His vengeance would be served upon that cursed temple; he had a drive that coupled with his knowledge of the dark arts, made him a force to be reckoned with. After discovering what had become of Lemuria, and knowing that the great crystal had gone with the meddling fools as he liked to call them, his plan had changed. Now, he was only going to be content with the city as his own, nothing else would appease him. He was aware of Macedon's work and he would reintroduce himself to him in time, for now he felt that it would be better to allow Macedon to continue unimpeded.

In the city there was a growing number of Atlanteans who were very discontented with the way in which their city was developing, secretly they formed an underground group, some of whom were ex-members of the shroud. Macedon and Kallicticus were aware of this group; however they were intrigued as to how it was going to develop, both for their own separate reasons. As it transpired, the meetings were unorganised and more destructive than constructive. There was a lot of shouting and accusations thrown around the room, yet the common denominator was that the group was going nowhere fast.

Eventually, word got to the group that there was a man who had done some work with crystals. It was suggested that he might be able to help with their development and focus. Word was sent out to try to find this man and ask for his assistance in developing the power that Hypatia had, it was felt that if they had this power they might be able to bring order to the city. It did not take long for Macedon to appear but he chose to remain in the shadows. Kallicticus would soon follow; his intention was to take over, expand the group and overturn the temple and city.

Macedon was uncertain as to whether he wanted to get too involved with this group of people, who would surely bring too much attention to themselves and therefore raise his own profile; in his mind he was sure that Kallicticus knew of this group if he was still in the city and if that was the case then he certainly wanted to avoid them at all cost.

With the triangle gone, as Kallicticus liked to call them, his purpose was gathering information to ascertain what effect it would have on the temple's influence over Atlantis. To his pleasure, it was soon apparent that Atlantis was suffering and it would not take much to assimilate the power of the temple and complete what his teachers had started. The only downside was the fact that the crystal was now gone. Much like Macedon, Kallicticus kept a low profile, he was not ready to assert himself as yet and was undecided about getting too involved with these people.

One evening in one of these secret meetings where there were many raised voices and accusations, a man stood up and declared:

"You people, with your accusations and name-calling have no idea of what you truly desire or how to achieve it." Kallicticus had heard enough and frustration had taken hold of him.

"Well please, enlighten us on how we can achieve whatever it is that we are supposed to be looking for."

This came from a bold man. He was the most outspoken of the group; he had a muscular appearance, which seemed to help sway the majority of the crowd and assumed leadership of the group.

"Firstly, what is your business here, as I believe that

you are new to this circle?"

"My name is of little importance at this time."

"Is that supposed to impress or scare me, because all I see is a little man with a big mo—"

But before he could finish that sentence, he was on the floor struggling for breath. Kallicticus made his way to the makeshift podium, stepping over the man without any regard.

"You wish to take power over the temple," Kallicticus said. "I am the way."

Kallicticus had waited patiently for the moment when he could exact his revenge on the temple; for dispensing with his masters. He had been watching Macedon since he had left the temple, in fear for his own life after the elders were crushed. Macedon had found a nice secluded place, in which he stayed in hiding. He had been left to his own devices, or so he thought.

Occasionally, Kallicticus would give Macedon boosts of energy when he felt low and lost in his work, which would give him the inspiration to make advancements in his work.

Now that he had the crowd's attention, Kallicticus laid out what he felt was the way forward. No soul would dare challenge him. He looked down at the muscular man who was still struggling for breath; with a wave of his hand the man was dead, now he was ready to begin moving towards the temple but first he had to let Macedon know that he had not taken his eye from all the members of the shroud.

The Lemurians were guests in a strange land, they had no explanation for what they had witnessed at the ascension. No one had been able to explain the strange series of events that had taken place, and the ascension had left them in a weakened state. They now feared the Atlanteans, as they had witnessed a power that was unforgettable.

Now the mass populace from Lemuria was becoming mistreated by the Atlanteans and was becoming a lower class, a situation that they brought onto themselves through fear of a race of people that seemed to have mystical powers, the Lemurians were losing their sense of pride. As for the Atlanteans they felt that the temple was losing control over the city, they felt that with the true power of the temple now gone, they could take better control of their own lives; the Lemurians seem to be subservient and it did not take long for this situation to be exploited. Some of the Lemurians had been approached by the discontented Atlanteans to do duties for them, as such, the servant class was established. It soon became the normality that if a Lemurian wanted to fit in, they needed to offer their services to the Atlanteans. So began the fall from grace of a once great civilisation.

Chapter Twenty-Five

The Rise to Power

Kallicticus was nobody's fool. He had a wealth of knowledge and power taught to him by the elders, and the wisdom of his masters meant that when the final judgement came, he would be well shielded. He was always working in the shadows; however, with the power of the great crystal gone, there was no need to hide anymore.

"All will know the man that is known as the lord," he said. "All will learn to fear my face."

It did not take long for him to take control of the new shroud. Six months has now passed since the ascension and it was clear now that Kallicticus and Macedon were working with one common goal, albeit separate, but the end result was always on the same path. Macedon would soon become the hidden force behind Kallicticus, who would impose himself on Macedon and felt he would have him in his pocket. As for Macedon, he had indeed managed to forge a crystal of immense power but the power was unstable and could not be contained.

Kallicticus knew that now was the time to start his advance on the temple. He went directly to Macedon's dwelling, a fact that took Macedon by surprise, he had long suspected that the goldsmith that did the temple work was in fact the lord and had hoped that he had managed to escape the hold that the shroud had over the members. His suspicions were confirmed when Kallicticus gave Macedon a full and detailed description of the work that Macedon had been doing, which included the crystal. Kallicticus knew that he had the answer to harnessing and stabilizing the crystal, and with the crystal in his control he would be all that his masters craved to be, and Macedon would be his puppet.

Macedon, however, had other plans; he trusted that Kallicticus had an end game, yet remained convinced that he was not a part of it. Because of this fear Macedon knew that he needed to produce a second crystal; he had learnt from his mistakes with the first crystal and over a period of time, managed to make a second which had more potency than the first, this one was more refined and purer. What he was not aware of was the fact that he was getting help from Hypatia, as this was always a part of the planned destruction of Atlantis, if the city could not resolve its destructive road that they now found themselves travelling on. He had learnt from the first, or so he thought, why it was so unstable and made sure that the second would be perfect totally unaware that it was Hypatia that was giving him the tools to do the work.

To offset the instability in the first crystal, Kallicticus used dark magic to control the crystal. In doing so, he also made sure that only he would be able to use its power. Now, everything was beginning to fall into place and he was ready to make his move. By now he had walked away from the organisation as he had no need for them, they were going nowhere fast and was beginning to attract unwanted attention to themselves that would hamper his advance.

***

Bion had served the temple well, a full year had passed and the priestesses had begun to respect him. The newly appointed head priestess had learnt to trust his judgement and advice, with the help of Petra, they were beginning to make a difference. As far as the ceremonies were concerned, he had not changed a thing. In fact, he even added some refinements brought over from his years in Lemuria which, when applied, made perfect sense and were implemented without any fuss or objections. The priests were happy with their newfound duties, as they were hoping that, that part of the temple would change.

The only downside was that higher knowledge of forewarning – in the form of Hypatia – was now gone. She would only instruct Bion in keeping with the path that was set, but it seemed that, that part of temple life was no longer needed. In time Bion had forgotten the warning that was given to him and was becoming complacent, a situation that was allowed to develop in preparation for his ascension, and that time had come.

"Bion, I bring you grave news," Ourania had linked into Bion. "Prepare yourself, my friend, for we are watching with great concern."

"What do you mean, things are good now?" Bion asked.

"You forget, Bion? Remember… remember now." Suddenly, he was presented with a vision in his mind that showed his destiny.

"Sweet goddess," he said. "How could I have been so foolish? Please forgive me."

"For what, you ask for forgiveness but you are only human."

In the distance he could now hear a lot of shouting coming from the central chamber direction, Bion froze for there were also objects being thrown to the ground and the priestesses were all screaming and crying, all but one.

Claritia had found the solitude of silence most comforting, when Gaia and Maeja left Atlantis she had not talked to a soul from that day until now. She remained in her chambers, it seemed only fitting to the temple that she be allowed to remain there.

***

At the time of the ascension, Claritia was informed as to the meaning of the call to gather and was given instructions by Hypatia.

"Claritia, wait here a while; we have not talked and I wish to converse with you now."

"Am I not needed at the gathering?" Claritia asked.

"No, you are needed here by me."

"What is your wish for me?"

"My wish, hmm… my wish is a hope that you, my child, will find comfort in what I am to tell you."

"You sound troubled, Hypatia."

"Claritia, you have been such a comfort to all that you have touched; it burdens my essence to tell you what I have to tell you."

"Hypatia, I serve to please, tell me what troubles you so."

"The time has come for us to leave," she said. "You know of what I am talking." A small tear began to form in Claritia's eyes. "Claritia, you know that this is hard for me, but when the time comes you will be called upon, for your journey is linked to ours and your part of this tale is not yet complete."

Now Claritia was listening intently. "Wait here," Hypatia said. "You are not needed at the ascension; we all love you, and we will be with you until the end." Claritia did not fully comprehend what Hypatia meant by that last statement, but it would be something she would come to understand and soon.

Hypatia floated down from her lofty perch and out onto the balcony. After Hypatia changed into her corporeal form and made her speech and the ascension process began, Hypatia came to Claritia.

"Prepare yourself, child," she said. "We have a gift for you."

What could this be? Claritia wondered, and then our souls appeared in front of her, as incorporeal silhouettes of our original form.

Maeja came up to her first: "Claritia, we will not leave you alone. We will give you a small piece of each of us, which will stay with you until the time comes that you are needed to help a dear friend to us all."

With that Maeja passed through Claritia; as she did, Claritia closed her eyes and kept them closed tight. With each soul that passed through her, she knew exactly who that soul belonged to. She could feel Maeja's strength and ferocity, Abraxas's wealth of knowledge and wisdom coupled with a memory of his home world and that feeling was amazing. She felt my kind heart and my never changing youthfulness; with every soul that passed through her, she smiled a deep smile filled with love and with every soul a new tear would fall. Everything seemed to stop, she opened her eyes and the only person that was standing in front of her was Hypatia. "This is our gift to you, this will see you through till the time comes; be strong, my child, we are with you always." Now she knew what it meant.

Hypatia now walked through Claritia; what she felt was so strong, so pure, that Claritia held herself but in her mind she was holding Hypatia, hugging her, silently thanking her. It was true unconditional love so strong, so pure, so fulfilling that for the first time in her life, she knew what it felt like to be in the womb of the creative entity that gave birth to all life. That was the last time Claritia talked.

***

On hearing the disturbance Claritia left her chambers, instinctively she knew it was her time, she didn't know how she just knew and calmly made her way to the central chamber. Bion had already entered the central chamber to find Kallicticus standing in the centre of the crystal circle and looking very pleased with himself. "Who in the goddess's name are you?" Bion demanded.

"Ah, high priest, and all this time I have been led to believe that you were a pussy cat. Had I have known you actually had a spine, I would have brought some protection." Then his tone changed, and his true nature came to the surface, at which point Bion could feel Ourania's and my presence.

"You dare challenge me, priest," Kallicticus said. "I have longed for this day. You will feel the weight of my vengeance, for your people will now feel the wrath of my fallen masters through my hands." Bion was still standing and with no ill effect.

"What is this? Why are you not on your knees dying at my feet? What power do you possess, priest?"

Suddenly, Claritia entered the room with an attitude and stance that was far removed from the person that she had become.

"You, Kallicticus, came into this sacred place without the knowledge of whom you are dealing with and expect us to fall at your feet. You will have this day and the days to come," Claritia said. "But you will not harm this man of the light." Bion was in shock.

This is the woman who cared for Hypatia and was at Gaia's side until the end, but has refused to speak since the ascension and now she commands the power of speech that would make a giant tremble? Bion's thoughts were backed up by a feeling that made the hairs on his body stand up.

Sweet goddess, it is Hypatia, Bion thought. *I feel her energy.* Claritia continued, unwavering with her stance.

"You, Kallicticus, have violated this temple. You will not get what it is you or your long-passed masters are seeking, you have sent this place to its doom. Relish in what you feel that you have achieved for it will soon turn bitter."

Claritia took Bion's hand, as she did so, Kallicticus lunged forward at them with a sword, which passed through them as if they were water. That was the last anybody saw of the high priest of Atlantis and the crystal keeper. Kallicticus was raging. He went through the temple killing all in his wake; within hours, the temple ran red with blood.

***

Petra had been told by Maeja that the time had come to go to Callus and get Zosimos and a small band of priests and priestesses out of the city, this was done the night before and Zosimos with his priests and priestesses were spared. They left Atlantis, eventually they would find their way with help to Agartha.

Chapter Twenty-Six

The Beginning of the End

Weeks had turned into months, so far Kallicticus was free of any retribution from the gods. He had truly asserted himself in his newfound glory and he had dispensed with anybody who could challenge him.

He kept Macedon close, as he needed him from time to time. Macedon had become quite skilled at producing crystals for Kallicticus. He in turn used magic to stabilise them, this enabled him to make quite a power centre in the temple. He had appointed disciples for his work and he had a closed chamber constructed, so he could hold sacrifices to the deities that he worshiped.

The elders would have been proud, he thought. *If only they were here to see it.*

In honour of his masters, all the priestesses were killed, leaving only men to serve in the temple. All of his planning had come to pass and he was happy with his work. Like Kallicticus of the past, Macedon was working in the shadows, he had attained enough knowledge of the different crystals to keep his work shielded from Kallicticus.

One morning, Kallicticus summoned Macedon to his chambers, whereupon entering, he found him wallowing in a bath of sweet smelling flowers. "Macedon, what have you learned of the tale of the Atlanteans that left the city many moons ago?"

"There was talk of a hidden city, but that is all I know."

"Have you not got crystals that can reveal their path?"

"The work that I am doing with those crystals has not borne fruit."

"Then try harder, I now grow tired of your petty excuses." With a wave of his hand, he dismissed Macedon from his chamber.

The fool tests my patience, Macedon thought.

Macedon was growing more resentful with each passing day; he would have to deal with Kallicticus, his time would come soon enough. The crystal that Macedon had created for himself was indeed a powerful source. He had managed to direct the crystal's power to create an underground complex of his own, much like the one that the elders had created. Kallicticus made a dangerous assumption in believing that Macedon was as loyal to him as he was to his masters. He didn't think that this unassuming man – who would not raise his voice much less his hand – could ever be in a position to threaten him. After all, he was the lord, so why would he waste his time keeping track of him.

In his underground lair, Macedon had a family of crystals, which were all capable of creating great harm. Due to his love for his creations, they were loyal only to him. He hadn't considered what had happened to the Atlanteans, as this was of no importance to him. His mind was firmly set on Atlantis, for there were riches to be had.

By now, some of the people from Lemuria had grown tired of being subservient to the Atlanteans and were beginning to do things for themselves; this was brought about by the overturning of the temple and this brought about an ethos that to take what you want is better than waiting for scraps. They had forgotten the ways of their people; as well as the mistakes that led to their downfall, their minds were now set on making riches through means and ways that were not fitting for this once great city. Their actions would have had the temple in an outrage. However, as the temple was no more and the man that was sat on a seat of power was no more than a murderer, it seemed that there was no control over how or what the population did. Control ceased to be the objective but the acquisition of wealth was all that the people were concerned about.

There were places of entertainment, where a man could pleasure himself on a woman and places where alcohol could be consumed... all of which, Kallicticus would profit from. Kallicticus was now the self-proclaimed leader of Atlantis. One merchant visiting the city had asked if he was the king of this land, a word that was foreign to Kallicticus, but one he liked nevertheless.

Macedon heard of this and was in a rage. *How dare he,* he thought. *That is blasphemy! This has to stop and stop now.*

Macedon set about preparing the temple; he had masked the crystals that he was going to use and placed them in strategic places, so that they would mask his master crystal from Kallicticus. The whole process took several weeks, as he had to be careful so as not to raise any suspicion from the appointed disciples, or Kallicticus himself.

Demeta had been keeping a close eye on the affairs of Atlantis. She was in talks with Timo, Ianthe, Petrus and Hypatia, to discuss what was happening there. It was upsetting to Timo and Ianthe, as this was their former home, but they knew that this was forewarned and it had to come to pass. Demeta would not have to interfere as she did in Lemuria, as they were set to destroy themselves. Timo had picked up the energy of the two crystals long ago and she had worried that if they were used incorrectly, then this could cause terrible devastation on the earth-mother. Demeta was well aware of Timo's concern, but assured her that she had help and not to worry.

"When these two abominations clash and they will, I will wash the land so as to remove the stain that is now Atlantis, but not until Agartha bears witness to what the misuse of power will do to a civilisation." Demeta was very passionate as she spoke.

Demeta linked in with an old friend, who was her silent partner. The emperor crystal was in danger because of the work that Macedon was doing. It seemed that Macedon was close to discovering the emperor and this was not acceptable. For Demeta to intervene, she had to have the emperor's permission.

"Demeta, I can feel you wittering away there and after all this time, you still approach me with care."

"Would you not show me the same respect?"

"Indeed I would, but in these troubled times, let us dispense with the formalities and get to the point," he said, matter-of-factly.

"Your location is in danger, there is one that wants your energy and for negative reasons."

"After all this time you come to tell me of what I already know, now you are to tell me that I must go to Agartha and confirm that the people there are respectful of our ways."

"If you know, why are you still here?" she asked.

"Waiting for the invitation."

"You will never change will you?"

"No, but just so you know," he said, "I already have my spot planned out."

Demeta laughed. "Of course you do; so now I may tell Timo."

"Ah Timo," he said. "I have heard good things about her. My friends are all eager for her to work with them."

Timo was in the now completed hall of power, which she would visit every morning while walking with Kallias. It seems that she could not get out of the habit of her walks with Maeja. She would tune into the crystals to check on them, as some of them were being used to generate the power grid for the ever-growing city. They had to be monitored and adjusted, so as not to put too heavy a strain on them.

Timo was in the chamber and could feel Demeta's presence. They had become close friends, much like the relationship I had developed with Hypatia.

"Greetings to you, Demeta," Timo said. "How is the world today?"

"As it should be," Demeta said. "How are you, Timo?"

"As well as could be expected, but I sense that there's something you wish to discuss."

"Yes, my dear, it is a matter of great urgency."

"When is it not, for it seems that Atlantis has demanded a lot from us these past days."

It was true that the activities of the would-be king, with his lust for power, were having a detrimental effect on Demeta and Timo. The work that had been done on the crystal was creating an imbalance in Demeta's power grid.

"Yes, that it has, and that is indirectly why I come to you now. I have a friend that is unknown to you. He is extremely old and has lived on this earth since its inception. The man who is doing the work on the crystals is becoming a problem, I fear that he may connect to my friend and discover him. If this happens and he manages to manipulate him, I will not be able to stop him."

"How is it that he commands that much respect from you, yet this is the first that I am hearing of him? And furthermore, what is his name?"

"He is simply known as the emperor."

"Who else knows of him?"

"He is only known by a select few."

"How is it that I have not heard of this before now?"

"He is a crystal and is very dear to me and to the planet."

Timo was confused, for she had the crystal that helped birth this planet. Abraxas had returned it after its use to dispense with the elders and Demeta could sense her confusion.

"They are not one and the same," Demeta said. "He is older than that particular crystal and has been around since time began. He will be arriving shortly."

"Who is bringing him here?"

"He travels of his own will."

"He can do that?"

"Yes that he can."

"Where shall I keep him?" Timo asked. "Will the hall of power be OK, or the hall of wisdom?"

"He tells me that he has his own spot, so I guess it will be up to him."

"Quite a wilful fellow then."

Demeta laughed: "You will find out just how wilful he can be."

It didn't take long for Timo to meet this mysterious crystal. She had been called to the hall of power and before she had arrived, she had picked up the energy that was coming out of the building. Kallias was not far behind her, he too had felt the surge of power.

"What is happening?" Timo demanded from one of the workers, who were running out of the building.

"It's the crystals... they started glowing and vibrating... we could not contain them."

Timo ran inside to see and Kallias followed close behind her. When Timo arrived in the main hall, she was reminded of Atlantis. All the crystals were illuminated and vibrating at such a high rate that she feared they would crack or explode. Timo went directly to the crystal that she felt would be able to give her answers as to why this was happening, but when she got to within two feet of the crystal, she was confronted with a field of energy that prevented her approaching any closer. This shocked her, never had any crystal refused her approach. Then, the earth began to vibrate.

"Demeta, what is happening here?" Timo demanded.

"I was waiting for you to ask; you took your time, Timo."

"I am in no mood for games."

"Remember your place, Timo."

"Apologies; I care about the people and the crystals equally, so please, enough with the games, do you know what is happening here?"

"All I will say is, say hallo to The Emperor."

Suddenly, the floor opened up and out rose a majestic crystal, which stood in the centre of the hall. He had settled in the spot that he found pleasing. He was welcomed by the crystals in the hall, by them giving unto him their light, he in turn gave it back, as that was their way. Timo approached him but before she could say a word, he spoke.

"You must be Timo, my friends have told me glorious things about you, but I will see for myself, as I will be watching you."

"Is he always this bold?" Timo directed her question to Demeta, as she felt that this crystal had not done anything to gain her respect.

"Usually more so to people he is not familiar with."

"Well, let him know that when he can show some level of decency, he may ask for me, and as for watching me, I don't take kindly to having either me or my friends watched or dictated to."

The emperor let out such a laugh that the walls shook.

"She has spirit; I like that, she will do just fine."

"Excuse me," Timo said. "To whom are you referring to, surely it cannot be me?"

Again, the emperor laughed. "Timo, may I be so bold as to tell you that I am a fan. I just needed to see how much you have grown since I put the labradorite onto your path, for that woman was, well, let's just say overwhelmed with the task that was set before her."

"You put my angel in my path?"

"Yes Timo, and he has kept me apprised of your progress."

"Were you aware of this, Demeta?" Timo asked.

"There is a lot that the emperor does that I am not aware of he is—"

"Be careful, Demeta." The emperor stopped her from saying what was not for her to say.

"I understand this game, but is there a name that I may call you? It would help."

"It would help with what, Timo?"

"A building of trust."

"If that is what you feel you need, then I will let you choose one for me."

"Thank you. I will think it over," Timo said. "So how may we help you?"

"It is I who will help you, Timo. Being here is of great importance and before you ask... no, Demeta was not aware."

Demeta made her excuses and left them to become better acquainted for she had important things to prepare. From that moment on Timo spent a lot of time in the emperor's company; they had plenty to discuss and it seemed that this crystal rivalled Hypatia. In the meetings that followed, it was revealed that the emperor was birthed at the same moment as Hypatia but where she was selected to be with the galactic command, he was selected to be a gate keeper, and this was not his first planet that he had responsibility for, and it would certainly not be the last. Timo found that she understood this crystal; she began to wonder if this was what it was like for me. As time went on, it was not long before she began to respect him more so then she respected Hypatia, the bond that these two souls had was getting stronger by the day.

"You know you will have to choose a name for me at some point," the emperor said. "I look forward to hearing what you will choose for me."

***

Macedon had spent many weeks in his cave, in Kallicticus's mind, he was seeking the answers to that which he so badly needed. He never told Macedon why it was so important that he had this information but Kallicticus was aware that Abraxas and I had left the city and returned just prior to his master's demise. We had returned with an object that aided us in his master's fate. He had spent the time that followed their demise looking for the missing Atlanteans but to no avail. Kallicticus sent his people out many times to bring Macedon to him, but they would return with the message that he was not in his den. Eventually Kallicticus became furious. Macedon, however; was refining his crystal, which had become so well balanced that it was now helping Macedon to this end. Together they had managed to help the crystal to levitate and appear to be invisible to the naked eye. This was the final piece of the puzzle and now Macedon was ready to meet Kallicticus and finish his finest work. He had learned that Kallicticus was looking for him, so he wanted to make him wait, for he knew that if he was unbalanced then he would be vulnerable and unprepared. He would make him wait another three days.

Macedon spent this time in deep meditation, linking in with the crystal, so that they would be linked in life and in death. He did not want Kallicticus to take his crystal if he should fail; if that happened, the crystal would vibrate at such a rate that would cause it to overheat and extinguish all in its path… in so doing ending the life of Kallicticus.

Chapter Twenty-Seven

The Final Breath

The wait was now over; it was time to face Kallicticus and, the goddess willing, rid the land of this evil man. Macedon left the protection of his hidden cave, the crystal had cloaked itself and followed Macedon out into the open. Before Macedon left the path that his den was situated on, he was greeted by two of Kallicticus's men.

"Where have you been? The king has been waiting for you, it is not wise to torment him so."

"That is not of your concern," Macedon said. "For I am going to him presently."

They followed Macedon at a distance, while the crystal was tracking them from a height that would avoid the contact of any passers-by, ever watching, ever protecting. Macedon was in no rush to get to the waiting would-be king, just the sound of it made him mad. Nevertheless, he had to stay composed and focused; he could not let petty-mindedness interfere with his mission.

Kallicticus was made aware that Macedon was seen and on his way to the temple, but he was growing impatient.

"Who does this fool take me for? I am no unimportant whelp, I am the King of Atlantis and he will give me the respect that my title holds." In a rage Kallicticus left the temple.

They met on the main stretch and immediately Macedon could sense his anger.

"You fool; you test my patience."

Macedon acted as though he was surprised at Kallicticus's rage.

"I was told you wished to see me. I came as soon as I heard."

"Now you take me for a fool!"

"Not so, but if you sent people you could trust, then maybe I would have been told sooner."

"I have not invested in you for you to mock me, Macedon, so tread carefully."

"My foot is always careful; it is you who should tread with care."

Kallicticus laughed.

"What is so amusing?" Macedon asked.

"I will kill you now, you insolent little man."

"You will do no such thing, Kallicticus, for I too have acquired power."

Kallicticus dug deep into his well of dark magic to give this fool such pain that he would wish for the sudden death. But nothing.

This fool hasn't trained as I did, Kallicticus thought. *What could he possibly know? Why isn't my power working over this fool that stands before me?*

Macedon cast a smile of victory: *Time for a little fun,* he thought.

"Impotency problems, Kallicticus? Shame it can come to us at any time," and with that said, Macedon's crystal shot a small beam of charged light at Kallicticus.

Not knowing where it came from, Kallicticus turned and ran. He needed his crystal and hoped that it wouldn't fail him. What he was not aware of was that Macedon's crystal had enveloped Macedon with a shield of charged energy that was difficult to penetrate. If not for that, Kallicticus would have been successful in his attempt to cause Macedon great pain; up to that point the shield was untested but Macedon had to test it before revealing his hand. He followed Kallicticus directly to the central chamber where his crystal was located, giving all his power to the crystal in order that it would kill Macedon. Kallicticus threw shot after shot at Macedon, yet he could now see that he was being protected by an unknown entity.

Macedon's shield was beginning to weaken but he had to maintain this for a little longer, long enough for Kallicticus's crystal to show signs of weakness. Macedon knew this crystal well and knew that it would not be able to maintain this continuous bombardment. And there it was… a little flicker, that only Macedon knew to look for. At this point Macedon linked in to all the crystals that he had placed around the temple, and they in turn linked in to Macedon's crystal, which gave the crystal the signal to reveal itself and also to give in to the crystal their reserved energy thus boosting Macedon's crystal to deliver Kallicticus his final fate.

Kallicticus could not believe what he was seeing, and wondered how Macedon could have done this without his knowledge? Now Macedon unleashed the full power of what he had created; shot after shot of highly charged energy was thrown at Kallicticus, and by the time it was over, Macedon was standing tall over a charred corpse. Kallicticus was dead but Kallicticus was no fool, he knew that it was the power of a crystal that had killed his masters, so when manipulating his crystal with the dark magic, he put inside the crystal the power to draw the power from any crystal that had the power to defeat him; that power would turn against that very same crystal, thus attacking it from within. Before Macedon realised what was happening, both crystals exploded, and he could do no more than watch his plan and life vanish before him.

Timo was in the hall of power talking to the emperor crystal about Agartha and the plans she had for the building of the city and the protection of its location. The emperor could feel the build-up of negative energy between these two abominations, but remained silent in order to see what the effect would be on Timo.

"Demeta, are you with us? Do you feel it? I know the emperor does." Now he was impressed. She had shown that she was getting more intuitive with the crystals in her vicinity, but was that where it ended? Yes, she had truly grown and was still growing, and she would make a fine ambassador.

"Yes, Timo, it's Atlantis," Demeta replied. "It will soon be time, prepare the city."

"Will it be you who dispenses the final judgement?" Timo asked.

"I am afraid it will always be me," she said. "They did have the chance to correct their ways, but weakness is its own punishment and the imbalance must be corrected. The people of Agartha will witness the final chapter of what is Atlantis, prepare the city, and I will allow them to see what has become of their people."

The word was put out for the people to prepare for a shift in energy, as the earth-mother had to rebalance the power grid of the earth. They were told to gather in the central square for the earth-mother would allow them to witness the ways that had led to this moment. When all were gathered, Demeta illuminated the ceiling of Agartha to reveal a link to Atlantis and the rise of her destruction. All that lived in Agartha knew exactly what this meant and how it would affect them, as the memory of the last time this was needed could never be forgotten. When the time came, Demeta moved one of her major plates to allow for a shift that rose the oceans to engulf that land formally known as Atlantis. However, unlike Lemuria, no warning was given and no one was spared, and as before, the people of Agartha felt great pain of such a loss. Some cried out with empathy, some prayed for the souls of those lost, but all felt the loss.

Epilogue

Life Continues

In my mind the treatment that I was receiving from Dr Graham had worked wonders, it had been more than five years that passed from when I first started to travel to a past that I never knew existed. All of the sessions were recorded, so that they would serve both patient and doctor for future reference. As for my nervous disposition, that had long been extinguished, but the journey had to be completed to its end. When it was quite apparent that my anxiety was no longer an issue, Eugene asked me if I would like to continue in order that we might finish what we started, I was eager to see how this story finished so was more than happy to continue.

In the office, however, I had lost my need to be alone and had found strength which was fuelled by my previous life as a high priestess, with nowhere to hide and a full acceptance of who I was. During the course of the treatment, I had been offered a promotion, which I accepted. I redesigned the floor and relocated fifty per cent of the staff, and as a result, the efficiency of the staff had risen one hundred per cent. I had the respect of the whole department, and the company directors noticed me as a person who could motivate her staff. The gossiping had stopped and all staff helped with the productivity of the department; all this was achieved without the need to employ harsh bully tactics.

It seemed that Chris Rogers was brought in to clear the way for me, but I needed to be tested and pushed to see if I had what it took to lead the team. His tactics were extremely harsh and there was a time when they feared that they would lose me. Eventually, they had learned that I was under psychiatric help, but in time I had begun to fight back in a manner that earned not only their respect but also the respect of my fellow workers.

It was mid-December and the directors were pushing for the pre-yearly reports so they could make their predictions and forecasts for the next quarterly business profile. Chris Rogers was the tip of the spear and I was the shaft.

"Antonia, where is the report that was promised three days ago?" he asked abruptly, Chris was not known for his politeness.

"The report is not complete; I am waiting for some final figures from the accounts department." I was flustered, but I tried to remain in control.

"Well, why was I not informed? Am I not the boss of this department?"

I did not respond although I wanted to; instead, I just walked away and went to the ladies' room to compose myself. Whilst there, I heard a small voice telling me to stand up for what was true. I ignored it, but then it spoke again… and then again.

I stood in front of the mirror and found myself actually saying the words, at which point Patricia Browning came out of one of the cubicles and looked at me with a smile of acknowledgement.

"Antonia, you know you have the strength to do the job," she said. "Don't let that bully get the better of you. Did you know that in times past we women had all the power and the men used to serve us? Think about that and take the power you need from the knowledge that you are a strong woman who deserves respect in this world, just like those men out there."

Patricia turned and left, leaving me feeling dumbstruck. Had I told someone of my therapy? Had I let something slip when I was in the toilet?

I rushed out to catch Patricia in the hallway. "Patricia, may I talk to you a moment please."

"Yes," she said. "How can I help you?"

"What you said in the ladies' room."

"Excuse me," she said looking bemused. "I haven't seen you in the ladies' room."

"You were just in there, and you said to me that I deserved respect."

"Antonia, whatever it is that you are on you need to stop," and with that, Patricia walked away.

I left work that day in a state of mild panic. That night I had confirmation that I was not going crazy and that I was closer to Gaia than I realised.

The following morning, I woke from a deep sleep, a sleep that I would never forget, for in the dream Maeja had visited me.

"It was I who visited you today, for you must wake up now and remember who you truly are. You are Gaia, born to serve under Hypatia and to serve the galactic command. The time has come for you to regain control of your life and remember who you are."

I returned to work that morning to be harassed by Chris for the reports; it didn't take me long to respond, fuelled by my visit from Maeja. I walked straight into Chris's office and told him in no uncertain terms.

"Leave me to get on with my job or do the report yourself," a job I knew he would not be able to. "And if you are not going to do that, then you can get hold of Accounts and tell them to surrender the reports that I need to complete my work. Now, be the manager that you are being paid to be."

I left his office, but to my embarrassment, the door had been left open and the staff were looking at me with looks that said, "Well done, girl." That was the day that I became the woman that I was meant to be… the day that my life truly began.

Over the years that were to follow, Eugene and I were instructed to continue our sessions, as it seemed that my higher self, my soul, wanted to share what transpired with my friends. I as Gaia had always kept a watchful eye on my friends. After all I was guardian to Earth, and so the story continues…

UNTIL NEXT TIME

Lightning Source UK Ltd.
Milton Keynes UK
UKOW04f2155220917

309708UK00001B/67/P